I0623251

MISTAKEN GIFTS

A Castle Mountain Lodge Romance

ELENA AITKEN

Ink Blot Communications

Also by Elena Aitken

Castle Mountain Lodge

Unexpected Gifts

Hidden Gifts

Unexpected Endings - Short Story

Mistaken Gifts

Secret Gifts

Goodbye Gifts

Tempting Gifts

Holiday Gifts

Promised Gifts

Accidental Gifts

The Castle Mountain Lodge Collection: Books 1-3

The Castle Mountain Lodge Collection: Books 4-6

The Castle Mountain Lodge Collection: Books 7-9

The Castle Mountain Lodge Complete Collection

The Springs Series

Summer of Change

Falling Into Forever

Second Glances

Winter's Burn

Midnight Springs

She's Making A List

Summit of Desire

Summit of Seduction

Summit of Passion

Fighting For Forever

The Springs Collection: Volume 1

The Springs Collection: Volume 2

The Springs Collection: Volume 3

The Springs Complete Collection - Books 1-10

Destination Paradise

Shelter by the Sea

Escape to the Sun

Hidden in the Sand

Ever After

Choosing Happily Ever After

Needing Happily Ever After

Wanting Happily Ever After

Fighting Happily Ever After

We Wish You A Happily Ever After

Keeping Happily Ever After

Finding Happily Ever After

Seeking Happily Ever After

Cherishing Happily Ever After

Ever After: Volume One (Books 1-4)

The McCormicks

Love in the Moment

Only for a Moment

One more Moment

In this Moment

From this Moment

Our Perfect Moment

Stand Alone Stories

All We Never Knew

Drawing Free

Sugar Crash

Composing Myself

Betty & Veronica

The Escape Collection

Vegas

Nothing Stays in Vegas

Return to Vegas

Timber Creek

When We Left

When We Were Us

When We Began

When We Fell

Bears of Grizzly Ridge

His to Protect

His to Seduce

His to Claim

Hers to Take

His to Defend

His to Tame

His to Seek

Hers for the Season

Bears of Grizzly Ridge: Books 1-4

Bears of Grizzly Ridge: Books 5-8

Halfway Series

Halfway to Nowhere

Halfway in Between

Halfway to Christmas

Chapter One

WITH ONE HAND, Eva Andrews navigated the snowy mountain road that led to Castle Mountain Lodge, while she reached for her cell phone and hit the Bluetooth button, answering the call. If Andi was with her, she would have lectured her about distracted driving, and yes, Eva knew she should probably focus on the road, but she never could ignore a ringing phone. It could be a client for their Party Hearty business, and making clients wait wasn't good business.

But it wasn't a client's voice that came on the line.

"Hey babe," Liam's confident and slightly cocky voice boomed over the speaker system of the car. Eva tried not to roll her eyes at the nickname he'd given her, but a small smile tugged at her lips, too. They'd only been dating a little over a month, but as independent as she was, Eva had to admit, she liked the way he took charge of any situation, even if it was with a lame nickname. Sometimes a girl liked to feel taken care of.

"Hey yourself," she said, her voice laced with flirtation. "It's about time you called me back. I still need an answer about next weekend."

"Remind me again," he said. "What's next weekend?"

Eva swallowed her sigh. "My friends are getting married, remember. Andi and Colin? I thought I'd mentioned it." She probably should have been more annoyed, but it was possible in all the planning she'd been doing for the big day, she'd forgotten to mention the fact that she wanted Liam to come up to the Lodge for the weekend and be her date.

It was a big step, but she wasn't getting any younger and he'd have to meet her friends sooner or later.

"Oh yeah," he said, "you did mention it and you know I'd love to meet your friends, babe. But—"

"But?" She shook her head, thankful he couldn't see her. Eva hated excuses. Everyone knew that. Liam knew that. "It better be a pretty important 'but' because it's a pretty important wedding."

Liam sighed, and started in on how busy he was and how he couldn't just sneak off for a weekend in the mountains whenever he wanted. Eva tuned Liam's monologue out as she concentrated on the road. The heavy clouds that had been threatening to let go finally had, and the snow was falling faster and heavier than she would've liked.

"So," she said, interrupting him. "Can you come?"

"Well, that's the thing, babe." He paused and the silence was heavy. "I don't think my wife would like it if I skipped out for a whole weekend."

The car swerved and Eva quickly righted it on the road. "Your wife?" she managed to choke out. She'd been expecting bad, but not a wife.

"Yeah, Bridgette. I was going to mention her, but I guess I didn't have the chance yet."

Eva's mind flew through the conversations they'd had. There hadn't been many, and she did have a tendency to tune him out when he started rambling, but still, she would've remembered a detail like a wife. "You most certainly did not," she said.

"It's no big deal, babe."

"No big deal?" Eva clenched the steering wheel and tried desperately to control her anger so she wouldn't drive herself into the snowy ditch. "I'd say having a wife is a pretty big deal."

"Are you mad?"

"Mad?"

"Yeah, are you mad? Because Bridgette doesn't mind. We have kind of an open—"

"Are *you* mad?" Eva hollered into the car. "Are you freaking insane, Liam? How can your wife not mind that you're dating me."

"It's not really dating though, is it? I mean, I thought we were just screw—"

"Don't say it," Eva said through clenched teeth. "Do not say one more word."

He was at least smart enough to listen to that piece of advice and silence filled the car, pressing down on Eva until she spoke through clenched teeth. "Don't you have anything to say for yourself?"

"You told me not—"

"Forget it," Eva said, and pushed the button on her cell phone, ending the call. "You're not worth it anyway," she said to the empty car.

None of them were. When it came to the men she dated, if it wasn't one thing, it was something else. She probably wouldn't know a decent guy if he walked right up to her and handed her a rose. But a wife? That was a new one. Eva hit the steering wheel with the palm of her hand, causing the car to swerve on the ice.

"Dammit," she muttered, and returned her focus to the road. There was no point dwelling on whatever it had been with Liam; it wasn't serious anyway. But the road conditions were. She clenched her fingers tighter on the wheel and concentrated on making it up the mountain to the Lodge without driving into the ditch. Andi sounded beyond stressed last time they'd spoken and Eva was pretty sure it would put her best friend over the edge if anything happened to delay her arrival.

"You're here!" Andi flew across the foyer and wrapped her arms around Eva before she had a chance to shake the snow off her coat. "What took you so long? I've been expecting you for hours."

Eva wiggled out of her best friend's grasp and took a step back. Andi radiated and her smile was contagious.

"I don't know if you noticed," Eva said with a gesture in the direction of the window. "But there's a blizzard out there."

Andi waved her hand in dismissal. "It's just a few flakes. It's January in the middle of the mountains—what did you expect?"

"Just once, I'd like to come up here in decent weather. Why is it that you're always having some party emergency in the middle of winter?"

Andi shrugged and took Eva's arm in hers. "Come on," she said. "Carmen will have your bags taken up to your room." They walked through the large timber-framed lobby, and down a hall that led to the banquet room. "I keep telling you to come and visit in the summertime," Andi said. "If you think it's beautiful with the snow, you should see it with the wildflowers blooming, and the sun sparkling on the pond. It's beyond magical."

Eva stopped short and stared at her friend and business partner who she knew better than anyone. "Are you feeling okay? Because I know it's pretty here and all, but it wasn't that

4

long ago when I never would have heard such crazy things come out of your mouth."

"I know, I know. But ever since—"

"Colin. I know," Eva said good-naturedly. "You're in love and that makes the world look brighter. And I'm happy for you." Andi raised an eyebrow and Eva quickly added, "I am." She squeezed Andi's arm. "I really am," she said again, this time looking in her friend's eyes.

After a moment, Andi wrapped her arm around Eva's shoulders and they resumed walking down the hallway towards the banquet room. "I know you are," she said. "And soon you'll know exactly how I'm feeling. I have a good feeling that this new guy. Liam, is it?" Andi glanced up, but without waiting for an answer, she kept talking. "I have a feeling that Liam might just be the guy that can handle you and finally make you settle down. Everything you've told me about him, he sounds like—"

"He's an ass."

"Okay." Andi drew the word out and shot Eva a look that she didn't miss. "Should I ask?"

"It's probably better if you don't." Eva shook her head and stepped into the banquet room. "I'm done with men." Eva could feel Andi's eyes watching her as she wandered over to a table and fingered the centrepiece. "We'll have to change these," Eva said. "They're far too Christmasey for a January wedding. If we go with a winter forest theme, they won't be—"

"You're not even going to tell me why?" Andi appeared at her side and took Eva's hand away from the poinsettias. "The centerpieces are fine," she said gently. "Now tell me. What's really going on?"

Eva looked at her friend and the kindness in her eyes. She missed their girl talk: sitting in the Party Hearty office dishing on the various boys she'd dated and why they would never do. Andi was always a good listener and Eva knew how easy it would be to spill everything. She longed to tell Andi that she was so envious of her loving relationship that it hurt. That she too wanted to settle down and find a man who was more than just a fling. A man who would complement her instead of stifle her, a man who would encourage her independence but make her feel safe and taken care of at the same time. A man, who... it didn't matter. Eva wouldn't say anything. Not with Andi's wedding looming. Besides, things hadn't been the same since Andi met Colin. Her friend was desperately in love with the man who showed her how magical the holidays could be, and fell in love with her in the process. Which was great. It really was, but at the same time, her friend was no longer capable of seeing how truly desperate the dating situation was for the average woman. Well, at least how desperate it was for her.

Eva shook her head and forced a smile she hoped Andi wouldn't see as fake. "There's nothing to talk about. I'm just so overwhelmed with ideas for your big day. And given the fact that you didn't really give me much notice, I don't have time for any distractions." She pulled her oversized portfolio from her tote bag and flipped it open. "See here?"

Eva pointed to a photo of white flowers, pinecones, a dust of what looked like snow, and twigs artfully arranged. The effect, although rustic, was beautiful and absolutely perfect for a wedding at the Lodge. Andi squealed, just the way Eva knew she would. She snatched the portfolio out of Eva's hands and dropped into the chair, where she began flipping pages and exclaiming over all the details Eva had thrown together in the past few days.

"You've thought of everything," Andi said when she looked up after a moment. "I can't believe you did this all in only a few days."

Eva shrugged and flipped her long blond hair over her shoulder. "It's not a big deal. After all, it's what I do. What we do," she added pointedly.

"I know, I know," Andi said. "I've been kind of absent

lately, but that will change after the wedding. I promise. It'll be your turn to have a little vacation. You deserve it. Especially with all this."

Eva brushed off the comment. She didn't need to take time off. Besides, Andi and Colin would probably want a honeymoon and she had her work to keep her busy. It's not like she was about to run off to a hot beach with some equally hot guy.

She shifted from foot to foot as she glanced around the room. She was starting to feel the familiar itch to get started with the planning prep. The banquet room was still decorated for the Christmas season that had barely wrapped up. It would take a solid day to strip it down and start getting it dressed for a wedding. And that was only if she had competent people working for her. She was about to ask Andi how many people she'd have from the Lodge staff to help her when Andi grabbed a piece of paper from the portfolio and held it up.

"This is perfect," she exclaimed. "Vows by the pond?"

Eva silently cursed herself. She hadn't been sure her ideas for the ceremony would work out and she didn't want Andi to get excited about something that might not pan out. "Well, as long as it's not too cold or a blizzard or something," Eva said. "Maybe we can have a back-up plan, too. We don't want your guests to freeze."

"No," Andi said. She gazed at the photo and said, "It'll be perfect. It's such a small wedding and it's kind of where our first date was."

"I remember. Ice skating," Eva said and added quickly, "Don't worry, I won't make you say 'I do' with skates on."

Andi laughed, but her smile faded quickly and was replaced with immediate tears.

"Andi, are you crying?" Eva knelt so she was face to face with her. "I told you, I'd never make you skate in a wedding dress. I was just—"

"No." Andi waved her hand in a weak attempt to dry her

tears. "It's not that. Sorry, I've just been so emotional lately with everything going on. I swear I'm bursting into tears all the time. It's ridiculous." She wiped her face with a tissue Eva handed her. "Thank you."

"Of course."

"No, I mean for everything. For all of this. I didn't plan on having the ceremony so soon, but when Colin proposed…and then being here again for the holidays, it just felt right, you know?"

Eva nodded even though she most certainly didn't know.

"I just don't want to wait anymore. What's the point, right?"

What was the point indeed, Eva thought. If she had someone who loved her the way Colin loved Andi, she herself might be inclined to break her self-assigned rule of never getting married. The idea had tempted her more than once lately, not that she'd admit it to anyone, but there was no point even entertaining the thought when she hadn't met anyone worth the effort in years. Not when all she'd had to choose from were men like Liam.

"I just had an idea." Andi sat up straight. "You'd probably really like Colin's friend, Troy. He's a successful businessman, something to do with paint, I don't know. But I do know he's cute and more importantly, he's single."

"I don't need a date."

"Sure you do," Andi said. "You can't fool me."

Eva froze for a second before grabbing the portfolio away from Andi. She flipped through the pages so she wouldn't have to look up and into her friend's eyes. Andi knew her too well, and the last thing she needed to worry about was Eva's love life. Especially if Andi knew that she'd actually like to have a love life. It was better if everyone, including herself, kept to the original plan of staying single and carefree.

"Come on, Andi." Eva forced a lightness into her voice.

"You know me. I don't do serious relationships. I'm more of a casual kind of girl. That's the way I like it." She flinched inwardly at the lie that was becoming hard to keep, especially from herself. "Now, can we get back to work? Do you have any other ideas for the ceremony? Because we should start nailing down the details."

There was silence for a minute and when Eva allowed herself to look up at Andi's face, she could see the uncertainty there. Thankfully Andi didn't push. Instead, she said, "I did have one idea that I think would work really well. Especially if we have the ceremony at the pond."

Eva flipped to a clean page and poised her pen over the page, waiting to take note.

"What if I arrived on horseback?" Andi asked.

"Arrived where?"

"The ceremony, of course."

"You?" Eva said. "You want to ride a horse in your dress? A stinky barn animal? In a gown? And here I was worried about you on skates."

Andi pushed back from the table and stood, pulling Eva up as well. "It'll be perfect. And seriously romantic. I'm sure there's a white horse in the stables." Andi got that look on her face and Eva knew she was already picturing herself on the horse. "You're going to need to talk to Jeff."

"Jeff?"

"He's the stable manager. You can work out the details with him."

"Horse details?"

"Yes, silly. Are you feeling okay? You look a little stunned."

Eva shook her head. Stunned didn't begin to describe it. "Andi, I don't know. I'm not really the best person to deal with that. I don't do horses."

That was an understatement. Just the thought of a smelly stable was enough to wrinkle her nose, let alone the idea of getting near one of the huge beasts. She'd only been on a horse once and that was enough. She'd been twelve, and at summer camp. Of course that story had a far from a happy ending, unless you call a broken arm and a lifelong distrust of sitting on any four-legged creature a happy ending. Horses were pretty enough to look at, as long as she didn't have to go anywhere near one.

"Please," Andi pleaded. "I know you don't love horses. But I really think it would be great and I just don't have the time to deal with the details. My dad and the boys are arriving in the morning and I need to keep them far away from my mom. I'll have my hands full just with family drama. I really need you."

"What about your dad's wife?"

"Roxanne?" Andi rolled her eyes and quickly added a sweet smile. "Oh, she'll be coming later. She said she couldn't bear to be in the mountains one day longer than she needed to be."

Eva gave her a conspiratorial grin and as they both knew she would, she nodded. "I'll take care of it," Eva said. Of course she'd do it. But it didn't matter what Andi said; best friend or not, she wasn't getting anywhere near an actual horse.

Chapter Two

JEFF MICHAELS LED CLOVER, a patient, dappled mare, out of her stall, through the stable and out into the crisp morning air. The sun was shining, making the fresh snow from the night before sparkle and flash in the sun. There was nothing more peaceful than the meadows after a fresh snowfall and peace is exactly what he needed to clear his head.

"Here you go, beautiful," he said to the mare as he let her loose into the fenced pasture. There weren't any trail rides scheduled for the morning, so whenever possible he liked to give the horses a bit of freedom and he liked to believe they enjoyed the fresh snowfall just as much as he did. Especially on a quiet morning.

It wasn't the same in the city, he thought as he scanned the white field and towering mountains that enclosed him. As much as Jeff had enjoyed the change of pace and the exciting opportunity of working on the movie set, there was something to be said for the serenity of the Lodge. It was his home, and he loved it. But he had to be honest with himself, too.

Jeff leaned onto the wood fence and watched the horses, letting his mind ponder the question he'd been rolling around for days. What if he took the job? As much as he loved it in the mountains, lately he felt more and more like he was spinning his wheels. And when would such a great opportunity ever come up again?

"Excuse me!" A voice startled him out of his silent reflection. "Do you work here?" a female voice called out.

"So much for peace and quiet," he muttered under his breath. He turned away from the horses he'd been watching and had to bite his bottom lip to keep from laughing.

A tall, blond, and he had to admit, striking woman was picking her way through the deep snow in black leather, very high-heeled boots. The kind of boots dreams were made of. Her red coat contrasted sharply with the snow and she reminded Jeff of the actresses he'd worked with on set. He suppressed a sigh. He'd just spent the last week dealing with the overindulged, pampered princess type and from his experience, when there was a prima donna involved, there wouldn't be peace for anyone. Especially him.

He watched her for a moment as she carefully tried to step through the snow he hadn't had time to shovel yet. The entire effect was quite comical, and he probably could have watched her for entertainment for a little longer, but when she slipped and fell backwards, landing on her behind, his upbringing got the better of him, and he launched into action.

With three long strides, Jeff stepped through the snow and was at the woman's side. "Are you okay?" He reached down to offer a hand up. If he thought she was beautiful from a distance, she was absolutely breathtaking up close. And every bit a city girl. A city girl who was very angry to be sitting in the cold.

The woman pushed his hand away. "I'm fine," she said with a huff. "No thanks to you." She pushed up through the snow and struggled to her feet. "Do you make it a habit to make people tromp through a snowbank in order to talk to you?"

Jeff took a step back. He hadn't expected such fire to come out of her mouth. "I'm sorry," he said after a moment. "I haven't had a chance to get the shovel out yet. I wasn't expecting anyone until after lunch."

"Well, I'm here." The woman used her black leather gloved hands to brush snow from her coat. She closed her eyes in an obvious effort to compose herself. When she opened them again, her tone had softened considerably. "I'm sorry," she said. "I shouldn't bite your head off."

Jeff leaned back and assessed her. The last thing he'd expect from her type was an apology. "It's fine," he said. "And hopefully you didn't land in anything besides snow." He couldn't resist adding the last bit. He tried to hide his smile, but the glare she shot in his direction told him he hadn't been very successful. He swallowed and cleared his throat. "I'm sorry," he said, trying to save the situation. "What can I help you with?"

She looked him up and down as if trying to determine whether he'd be able to help her with anything at all. After a moment she said, "I need a horse."

Jeff tucked his hands into the pockets of his fleece-lined denim jacket. "Well, you came to the right place then. I think I have a few of those around here." He knew he was antagonizing her, but it was too tempting and he could use a laugh before he got down to work.

The woman crossed her arms in front of her chest and tossed her head back so her hair fell down her back. She narrowed her pretty blue eyes before she spoke and Jeff had the distinct impression that she wasn't quite as entertained by the situation as he was. "As fun as this has been," she said, "I really don't have much time. I'm looking for Jeff. I was told he actually knows what's going on around here."

The opportunity to continue to mess with her head was

tempting, but by the look on her face, Jeff was pretty sure he shouldn't push it too much further. He stuck his hand out and said, "I'm Jeff. It's nice to meet you..."

Her glare faded but she didn't uncross her arms and after a moment, he dropped his hand.

"You're Jeff?"

"The one and only."

"Great." She closed her eyes briefly and took a deep breath. "I need a horse," she said.

"We've already established that I have some of those," he said and waved his arm towards the meadow. He flashed her what he knew was a brilliant smile, but she didn't seem affected, so he settled into business. "Are you looking for a trail ride?" he asked doubtfully. He'd seen some interesting outfits on the guests before, but nothing quite as impractical for riding as what she was wearing.

"Me?" She dropped her arms and alarm flashed in her eyes. "Oh, no. I'm not getting anywhere near one of those..." She waved her hands in front of her face. "Beasts," she finished. "No way. I need one for the wedding."

Jeff surprised himself by feeling a flash of what had to be disappointment that she was engaged to be married.

"Do you mind me asking why you want a horse for your wedding? I mean, you don't seem to like them very much."

"Me?" Horror crossed her face. "No, it's not for me. I'm not getting married."

A wave of relief washed over him, shocking him further.

"Then..."

"It's for my friend's wedding in a few days. You don't know about it? How could you work here and—"

"I've been away working and I just got back last night. I did hear something about a wedding," he said, remembering the memo he'd seen on his desk. "But if I'm not quite up to speed, I'll have to apologize."

14

"Apology accepted."

He was about to shoot back a smart comeback when he saw her small smile.

"It's my friend Andi's wedding."

"Andi and Colin?" he asked, remembering the couple he'd had the pleasure to meet a few times in the past. "By the way, they're horses, not beasts," he added. The still unnamed woman may have softened her attitude a little, but he wasn't above helping get the point across, especially if he could make her pretty face flush again.

She ignored his comment, and said, "Yes. Colin and Andi's wedding. Andi's decided she needs to ride a white horse to the ceremony. She seems to think it will be a beautiful entry and since I'm her party planner and best friend, I need to make that happen. Now, please tell me you have a white horse?"

Listening to her, all the pieces fell into place, although based on the way Andi had raved about her best friend and business partner, he was not expecting the diva who stood before him. "Wait, you're Eva?"

"Yes. Who else would I be?" She stamped her feet in the snow, and shivered. Her feet must be frozen in those completely impractical boots.

"Well, I wouldn't know," he said. "Since you missed that small detail during our introductions."

He held out his hand again. "It's nice to meet you, Eva." This time she took it and even through her glove, Jeff could have sworn he felt the heat of her hand. He held the grip a moment longer than he should have, and then said, "I don't think I can help you, though."

Eva pulled her hand away. "With a horse?" She pointed in the direction of Clover and the other horses in the field. "You have some right there."

"Obviously I have horses," Jeff said. "But not for a wedding. No way."

He watched as her pretty face knitted up into a scowl. "Look," she said, some of the fire in her voice returning. "I don't get it myself. Riding a horse in my wedding would not be my first choice. But it's not my wedding, it's Andi's. And if she wants a horse, she's damn well going to get one."

Jeff shook his head. He'd seen one too many weddings go badly because of an inexperienced rider, already nervous, atop a horse that wasn't properly prepared. "No. It's policy. I will not be responsible for ruining a wedding."

Eva clearly wasn't used to hearing the word no. She glared at him, the effect ruined by a violent shiver that ripped through her body. "Oh, no," she said through chattering teeth. "I will get the horse."

Used to dealing with stubborn horses, Eva's stubbornness was an entirely different challenge. But they couldn't stand in the yard all day, not if she was going to freeze to death. "Why don't you come inside and warm up? You're not really dressed for the weather."

Eva looked like she might say no and he was surprised when she nodded and started to walk towards the large round building that housed his office in one corner.

She slipped in the snow and Jeff reached down, stabilizing her before she could fall into the snow again. "Let me help you," he said. "You know those aren't really the best boots to be wearing out in this snow." Even if they did make her legs look fantastic, he thought.

"I didn't expect to be schlepping around through a snow-bank," she said. "I didn't expect to be leaving the Lodge at all or I assure you I would have packed for the occasion." To his surprise, she didn't shake him off, but instead clutched his arm while he led her through the snow. Even more surprising was that the weight of her on his arm felt really good.

"Is that better?" Jeff asked Eva as soon as they were settled with a coffee mug in each of their hands.

She sipped at the steaming drink but didn't say anything right away. By the look on her face, Jeff couldn't tell if she was irritated with him or just frozen from the waist down. It was probably safer to wait until she made the first move.

It took half a cup of coffee and another few minutes to pass before Eva spoke. "Thank you," she said. "I didn't realize how cold I was." Now that she was thawed out a little, her demeanor seemed to have melted even more and while he couldn't be certain, Jeff thought he might have seen a glimmer of a smile, or what at least wasn't a scowl, aimed in his direction. And he liked it.

"Once you get your feet wet, it doesn't take long for the rest of you to freeze up," Jeff said. "It helps to dress for the weather." As soon as the last few words were out of his mouth, he wanted to pull them back. Especially when Eva's face closed up. They definitely weren't getting off on the right foot. "What I meant was, in this kind of weather—"

"I told you," she interrupted him. "I didn't expect to be tromping through a snowbank this morning, or I would have dressed for it. I do know what snow is." She took another sip of her coffee, but her eyes didn't leave his.

Jeff tapped his fingers on his desk and considered his options. It would be far easier to work with her if she wasn't angry all the time; besides, city girl or not, now that he had a look at that beautiful smile, he wanted to see more. "Look," he said, extending an olive branch. "I'm sorry the walk wasn't cleared." She relaxed a little, so he kept talking. "And I'm really sorry I didn't help you out. That's not usually my style. Can we start over?"

She seemed to consider his words for a moment. But finally she nodded. "I think that's a good idea. Believe me when I say, the last thing I wanted was to come to the stables."

"Well, you're here now," he said, certainly glad she was.

"Despite what you said, I need to order a horse for the wedding."

"Even if I did agree to it, which I'm not likely to," he said, "it's not like ordering a pizza, you know?" He tried not to laugh. "Besides, you could have just called. You didn't have to actually come down here."

Eva tilted her head and her long hair fell to the side over her shoulder. "You just said it wasn't like ordering a pizza," she challenged. "Besides, I like to see what I'm getting. So, how do I do this? Do you have pictures or something for me to look at?"

The laugh he'd been holding in escaped. "You want to order from a catalog?" Jeff sat up and pushed back from the desk. She couldn't be serious.

"No," she said. "Not like a catalog or anything. But photos or something," she said. "You can't tell me you don't have any pictures of your horses. A guy like you, you probably have them framed all through your house, don't you?" She crossed her arms and grinned. He didn't even want to see how obnoxious she would be if she knew she wasn't far off the mark. Jeff did have photos of his favorite horses, but not around his apartment or anything. Just on his phone. But she did not need to know that.

"Besides, it doesn't matter." He took a deep breath and exhaled slowly. "Because I'm not giving you a horse for the wedding."

Her face flushed again, and she clenched her teeth.

Without giving her a chance to argue, he added, "I won't be responsible for anything going wrong. It's too risky."

Eva let out a long breath and straightened her shoulders. "What if it wasn't risky?" she asked after a moment of thought. "I mean, for someone inexperienced, sure. But for Andi...she's been on horses before. It wouldn't be as risky."

He thought about what she'd said. Andi and Colin were more than guests at the Lodge; they were friends. And Jeff himself had personally led Andi on a number of trail rides. She'd probably be fine. And for friends, Jeff could break his "no horses in weddings" policy. But maybe Eva didn't need to know that right away. He took a moment and looked at Eva and how incredibly gorgeous she was when she was frustrated. She was so completely opposite of everything Jeff ever looked for in a woman, but there was no denying how much he was enjoying the challenge of their banter. He wasn't ready for it to end. "I'll consider it," he lied.

"You'll consider it?" She tipped her head, evaluating him. "Fine," she said after a moment.

"But why don't you tell me what you're looking for and I'll see what I can do. You know, just in case I decide it's okay," he added quickly. "Didn't you say something about wanting a white horse?"

For a moment, Eva looked like she was going to retaliate with another smart-ass comment, but then she swallowed and said, "Yes. Andi thought a white horse, with her wearing a white dress, would be dramatic. Do you think you have one that'll work?"

"I might be able to find one," he said. Jeff knew exactly which horse would be perfect for Andi, but something stopped him from telling Eva that. "I'll have to check. But I have to tell you, I don't think it's a great idea."

Eva put her coffee cup on the table and started to re-button her coat. "When will you know?" She barely glanced in his direction. "I'll need to come up with a back-up plan if you can't come through for me on this."

"I'll have to think about it," he said as he stood up. "But I'll let you know soon."

"You're sure?" She stood and shot him a look. "This is

Andi's wedding. I can't just depend on your vague word that you can make it happen. I need a guarantee."

"I said, I would—"

"Look, I have a lot to deal with right now. Please make sure you can deliver on this." Eva took two steps towards the door before spinning around. With a small smile on her face and a twinkle in her eye that Jeff couldn't figure out, she said, "I don't have time to play games, horse guy."

In a whirl of red, she was gone, leaving Jeff to stare open-mouthed after her. Did she really just call him "horse guy"? He laughed. Maybe his first impression was wrong. Eva was definitely not the Hollywood princess he'd seen so much of; there was no doubt she was different. But figuring her out—that would be something else. It was a good thing Jeff liked a challenge. Especially a beautiful one.

No. He shook his head in an effort to clear her out of his head. He didn't have time to mess with some prissy, overindulged city woman. Been there, done that. It never worked. And like her, he didn't have time to play games either.

He slid the envelope with the offer from the production company towards him. He had bigger things to think about. Like his career. According to the contract, he only had a week to decide if he was going to take the offer. And it was a good one.

Jeff let his gaze drift out the window to the snow-covered meadow where Clover and the other horses were nosing through the snow. Taking the offer would mean leaving the Lodge and the stables. He didn't know if he could do it. No, he didn't have time to play games with anyone, even if she was beautiful and more than just a little intriguing. He had a decision to make. And it wouldn't be an easy one. Jeff shoved the envelope into the top drawer of his desk, grabbed his leather gloves and headed back outside.

Chapter Three

EVA WAS STILL AMPED up when she got back to the main building of the Lodge twenty minutes later. She'd never considered the possibility of not getting a horse for Andi. She'd never been in a situation where she couldn't deliver on an event and even if she personally thought having a horse at a wedding was insane and just asking for trouble, if Andi wanted a horse, she'd get a horse. Even if it meant having to deal with Jeff and his ridiculous "no wedding policy." She'd get it done.

And dealing with Jeff wouldn't be that bad, Eva thought. Sure, he'd pushed all her buttons and completely tested her professionalism, but she'd gotten a few jabs in, too. And even if he was a horse guy, he was a seriously attractive horse guy. If you liked the muscly, big type. Which she did.

"No." Eva shook her head. There was no time to think about men, especially one who seemed determined to make her crazy. No, she'd keep her interest in him purely professional, just long enough to get what she wanted. Or in this case, what Andi wanted. They'd planned dozens of parties together, but none so important as Andi's wedding. And she wouldn't let her down.

Eva opened the door to her room and shrugged out of her coat. She also tugged off her leather boots, which were probably ruined from the deep snow, and God knows what else she might have stepped in out there. She rubbed her feet between her hands in an effort to restore some warmth, but only gave herself the luxury of a few minutes to sit before she dug out another pair of shoes, jammed her feet in them and headed back downstairs.

There was too much work to be done to let herself rest, and she definitely didn't have time to think about Jeff. Even if there had been something behind his arrogance that sparked within her so she couldn't get him out of her head. But no, she'd sworn off men. Especially men like Jeff. She'd dated enough to know that type. All muscle, like they spent all their spare time in the gym, or probably lifting bales of hay, in Jeff's case. Regardless, men who looked like that always had an over-inflated opinion of themselves and expected women to be lining up to go out with them. But not her. No way.

Eva passed through the lobby and gave a wave to Carmen, her friend working at the front desk. Maybe she would have time to grab a drink with Carmen later. No doubt Jeff had dated every woman at the Lodge, and Carmen would definitely know the details. That is, if Eva cared. Which she didn't.

Just thinking about him had her temperature rising, but she couldn't be sure if it was in frustration or something else, like the shiver she'd felt when he touched her. The shiver that had nothing to do with the cold. Eva stopped in the middle of the hall, took a deep breath and straightened her sweater over her skinny jeans. She couldn't remember the last time she'd gotten so worked up over a man. Eva prided herself on her professionalism, but Jeff had tested her at every move. Her face flushed at the memory of the way she'd behaved towards him.

She continued to the end of the hall and with one hand on the door to the ballroom, she paused again. Maybe she had been a bit hard on Jeff. After all, he hadn't hit on her, not really, and it wasn't fair for her to judge him based on her recent bad luck with men. And it wasn't Jeff's fault that he happened to work with horses, which she herself hated. Besides, maybe if she apologized, she'd be able to sweeten him up enough to let her have the horse for the wedding?

With a sigh, Eva shook her head so her hair cascaded down her back. "Fine," she said aloud and pushed open the heavy wood door. "I'll apologize."

She stepped into the room and walked smack into a man who put his hands up just in time to grab Eva's arms and keep her from running full force into his solid chest.

"Apologize to me?" the man asked. His eyes twinkled with humor.

"No," she said. Eva took a step back and adjusted her portfolio while she took a good look at the man. He was lean, not nearly as bulky as Jeff, but handsome with a full head of sleek blond hair. Everything about him was well-groomed and he just screamed successful businessman. Eva smiled in a flirting reflex. "But it seems I do have to extend an apology to you as well. Are you okay?"

He brushed off her concern. "I'm fine. I shouldn't have been standing in front of the door. And between you and me, I really shouldn't even be in here, but I couldn't help it. I had to see what type of decorations Andi was doing for the wedding."

Eva squared her shoulders and tipped her head. "You know Andi?"

"Of course. Well, to be fair, I've only met her a few times, but I'm tight with Colin." He smiled a grin that exposed a perfectly straight and white smile and extended his hand. "I'm Troy. And I have a feeling that you must be Eva. She told me all about you."

"Oh, you're Troy." She took his hand and then without bothering to hide it, she looked him up and down. Eva had to

23

admit, Andi was right when she said he was cute, in a Ken doll kind of way with his perfectly trimmed blond hair and blue eyes. Nothing like Jeff's rugged good looks, but cute. Eva couldn't stop the comparison from playing in her head.

"Do I meet your approval?" Troy asked. "Andi warned me about you." His smile reached his eyes and despite her annoyance with the male species in general, Eva found herself playing along with his teasing.

"I suppose you'll do."

"I'll do? I didn't realize it was an audition."

"Isn't it always?" Eva said, and returned his playful smile. There was something about Troy that was a lot of fun. Besides, after her run-in with Jeff, it wouldn't hurt to have a little fun with a man instead of sparring with him. "And knowing my best friend, I'm sure she mentioned my lack of a date for their big day."

"She may have mentioned it." He crossed his arms over his chest and leaned against the wall.

"And?"

"I don't think I'm the right guy for the job."

Normally, Eva would be offended, but Troy delivered the words with a lightness that somehow softened the blow, and she could tell there was more behind it.

"Why is that?"

"Because I'm gay."

The second the words registered, Eva burst into laughter. "I knew it," she said.

"You did not. You were checking me out."

Eva wiped tears of laughter from the edges of her eyes. "Okay, I'll admit, I didn't know. But with my luck lately, if you were straight, you would have found a way to irritate me the second you opened your mouth. So I knew something had to be different."

"That I didn't irritate you right off? Well, then that's a difference I'm glad to have."

"Me too," Eva said. "But I do have to disagree with you. I think you'd make the perfect date for the wedding." The thought of having to deal with an actual date was more than she could handle. Jeff's face flashed in her mind. But before she could think about what that meant, she said, "Do you think you could handle it?"

He assessed her for a moment. "You know what? I think I could."

"Perfect," Eva said. And he was. "There's just one more thing," she added. "Why would Andi want to set me up with you if you're gay?"

"I'm pretty sure she doesn't know. Well, she's never asked, and like I said, I've only had the pleasure of meeting her a few times, so I'd have to assume she doesn't know."

She dropped her portfolio on a nearby table. "Do you think we could keep that between the two of us?" If Andi thought she was with Troy, she would leave her alone about getting a date and then maybe she'd be able to have a little peace, at least for a few days.

Troy shrugged. "I don't see why not."

Eva nodded and with the matter of her date out of the way, her attention immediately shifted towards the decorations and what she still had to do. Which, by the looks of the room, was almost everything. The staff had removed the holiday decorations, but they hadn't begun any of the preparations for the wedding reception yet, which meant not only would she have to finalize the details of the ceremony, dinner, and party, but she'd also have to oversee the decorating. If only she had someone to handle it for her. With a sigh, she spun around and faced Troy again, her mouth working into a smirk as an idea came to her.

"So," she said slowly, "if you don't know Andi all that well yet, I suppose she didn't have the opportunity to warn you about my knack for putting people to work when I find them hanging around."

With Troy in charge of hanging white fabric on the walls of the ballroom and stringing twinkle lights throughout the room, Eva headed into the kitchen to take care of what was likely to be the easiest thing on her to-do list. Bruno, the head chef at the Lodge, was one of the best around and she knew whatever he decided on, it would be amazing and Bruno would likely outdo himself.

She hadn't had time to consult with Andi on her food choices, but knowing her the way she did, it wouldn't be too hard to nail down a menu. After all, Andi had put her in charge. There was no point bothering her with minor details.

Eva found Bruno chopping a pile of vegetables and tossing them into a pot. "Hey, Bruno. Have a minute to talk wedding food?"

Bruno glanced up, a smile spreading across his face from under his bushy moustache. "Eva. It's so good to see you." He wiped his hands quickly on a towel and wrapped his arms around her. It was a little like hugging a pole—Bruno was all bones—but the hug was familiar and it was always nice to see an old friend.

"Bruno, haven't I told you what they say about never trusting a skinny chef?" she teased him and leaned up against a prep counter as he got back to work.

"They can say whatever they want, my dear. You and I both know that what comes out of this kitchen is the finest food in the Rockies."

"That's the truth," she agreed. "I don't want to interrupt, but do you have a few minutes to get the menu planned?"

"Sure," he said. "If you don't mind me working while we chat." He picked up his knife again and started slicing through a carrot.

Eva snatched a carrot from the cutting board. "What about beef?" Eva asked before taking a bite. "Andi and Colin both like steak. Maybe a tenderloin or something?"

"Can't do it," Bruno said without looking up.

"What? Why not? Beef is always a crowd pleaser."

"That's what I thought, too," he said. He tossed the vegetables into the pot. "But Andi said no beef."

Eva almost choked on her carrot. "When did you talk to Andi?"

"Yesterday. She sent back the steak I cooked for her last night. Medium rare, just the way she likes."

"She sent back her steak? Andi never sends back food."

"Well, no one ever sends back my food." He looked affronted and Eva could imagine his anger at having his food rejected. "So naturally, I went to speak to the customer."

"Naturally," Eva said.

"It was Andi. She apologized but said it tasted 'off.'" Bruno slammed his knife onto the cutting board. "Off. Can you believe it? As if I would serve any food that was less than one hundred percent perfect." He wiped his brow with the towel and tossed it into a nearby laundry bin. "I'm sorry," he said and straightened his apron. "I'm just not used to complaints. And the steak wasn't off. I tested it to be sure. It was fabulous. The best cut in the house."

"I'm sure it was, Bruno," Eva assured him. "She probably just wasn't in the mood for steak last night."

"Or any night," he said. "She told me there was to be no beef served at the wedding. None. Can you believe it?"

Eva closed up her portfolio and snatched another carrot. She couldn't believe it. Andi had never been a picky eater, and more than that, she would never send food back to the kitchen. Especially Bruno's food. Something had to be wrong.

"I'll check it out, Bruno. I'm sure there was a mistake. That doesn't sound like Andi at all. I wouldn't worry about it."

"How can I not? I cannot have food sent back. It will ruin me." He threw his hands up in the air. If anyone ever thought chefs weren't prone to the dramatic, they'd never met Bruno before. "I can't have it, Eva. If she hates my cooking, maybe someone else should prepare the food for the wedding."

Leaving her things on the counter, she grabbed his arms and forced him to look her in the eye. "You're being silly," she said. "And you know it. Just relax and I'll take care of Andi and the food. Let's give her some choices. Maybe a nice chicken dish? And a salmon. Can you come up with those?"

He nodded and for a second Eva was afraid he would cry.

"Good," she said. Eva scooped up her portfolio, making a note to check on Bruno tomorrow after she spoke with Andi and could figure out what the hell was going on. "I'll see you soon and we'll make the final choices. I'm sure Andi was just having an off day."

She turned to leave, but before she did, she said, "Oh, and Bruno?" He looked up and met her eye. "I've never had a steak cooked as perfectly as yours."

When he burst into a broad smile, she winked and left him to his chopping.

Chapter Four

THERE WAS ONLY one girl who could turn Jeff's bad day into a good one. She had the purest blond hair he'd ever seen, features that looked like they belonged on a doll and a voice that made his heart sing. And the second he set foot in the cottage, she ran at him full blast.

He caught her in his arms and swung Ella around, making her squeal. The little girl had captured his heart when she came to live with her father—and his best friend—Bo over a year ago. A silent, withdrawn little girl, the only way to make her smile had been to take her for a ride on his horses, and it was that instant connection that had bonded the two together.

After that, once Ella had settled into life at the Lodge, and Bo had settled down with Morgan, Ella became something like a little sister or a niece to Jeff. It didn't matter which; he loved her more than anything and she was one of the strong pulls keeping him at the Lodge.

"Hey squirt," he said, putting her down on the rug. "Have you been good for your mom today?"

Ella rolled her eyes. "I'm always good," she said. "You know that."

"It's true," he said. "But maybe one day you'll surprise us all. Although I hope not." He took her hand and let her lead him through the small front room of the converted caretaker's cabin, and into the kitchen.

"What don't you hope for?" Morgan asked as the pair entered the kitchen. She put down the jug of milk in her hand and gave Jeff an easy hug.

"I was just telling Ella that I hope she never grows up."

"That's not what you said." Ella slapped him on the arm and giggled when he winked at her.

"Why don't you go and play for a bit before dinner?" Morgan suggested to Ella. "Either that or I'm sure I can find something for you—"

She didn't even need to finish the thought before Ella disappeared into her bedroom and Morgan turned to Jeff. "I was just making myself a cup of tea. Do you want one?"

"Sounds great," he said and settled into a kitchen chair. "Is Bo around?"

"Sorry," she said and turned back to the counter, grabbing two cups and a package of teabags. "He had a meeting with the general manager this afternoon. Something about some of the new treks he wants to offer this season. He must be running late. But I expect him back any minute."

Jeff fiddled with the placemat, rolling the fabric between his fingers. "No problem," he said. "I can always catch him later." Jeff watched as she poured steaming water into the mugs and brought them to the table.

"At least this way I get to hear all about your brush with fame before he does," she said. "I want to know everything about your trip. Were the actresses total divas? Did you get your own trailer? What was it like? I want details."

He couldn't help but laugh at her eagerness. "I never pegged you for the star-struck type, Morgan. You really want to know everything?"

"Oh, come on, Jeff. You know I love it up here but sometimes a girl needs to be reminded of the world outside of the Lodge. And Hollywood? Right in our backyard? Come on, you know I want to know."

"Well, it was pretty exciting," he said. "Especially the time when…" Jeff added a splash of milk to his tea and stirred as slowly as he could before he continued, knowing it would make her crazy.

"What?" She leaned forward, anxious to hear him spill his secrets of the stars.

"The time when they needed two horses on set instead of one," he finished.

"Jeffery Michaels, that is not funny." He looked up, right as she lobbed a tea towel in his direction.

"Honestly, Morgan. It was fun and different, but there really weren't any major brushes with fame. I mean, it was a television pilot, not a Hollywood blockbuster." When her face fell, he added, "Although they're saying the male lead, a Gage Mitchell, could be the next Brad Pitt. Maybe I could get an autograph for you next time."

Jeff caught the slip the second it was out of his mouth. He hadn't meant to say anything yet about the possibility that there would be a next time for him. But if the show got picked up, which was looking likely, Jeff knew it was only a matter of time before Marianne Marshall would be knocking on his door to be the on-set horse wrangler. She'd given him a week to look over the contract, but Marianne wasn't the type of woman to sit back and wait. Not even for a week. She'd need an answer in the next few days, and he still didn't know what it would be.

"Next time?" Morgan tilted her head and waited. "Are you going back?"

"Going back where?" Bo asked as he entered the kitchen. He dropped his jacket over the back of a chair and pulled Morgan into an embrace that made Jeff look away.

"Get a room," he said and focused on his tea.

"This is our room," Bo said with a laugh. "What's up, buddy? Have you become a big star yet?"

Bo grabbed a beer from the fridge and handed it to Jeff without asking if he wanted one. He took one for himself before sitting down at the table as well. "Cheers," Bo said. "Welcome back."

Morgan made a face at them and took a pointed sip of her tea. "Jeff was just telling me about the next time he goes on set," she said.

"You're going back?" Bo took a swig of his beer. "I thought it was a one-time deal. A pilot or something."

Jeff took a deep breath. There was no point keeping it from his closest friends, but somehow, talking about it out loud would make it real. Which meant he'd have to make a decision. And that was the whole problem. He was pretty sure he already knew what his decision would be. "It looks like the show will be picked up. And it's not official yet. But according to the producers, it's in the bag so they're starting to sort out their staff."

"And let me guess," Bo said. "They want the best horse wrangler in the country on set?"

"They've made me an offer, yes," Jeff said. He tipped the beer back and took a long drink so he wouldn't have to meet Morgan's eyes.

"That's great." Bo put his beer down and let out a small whoop of triumph. "What a great opportunity."

"How would you manage your time between the set and the Lodge?" Morgan asked.

Jeff didn't even have to look at her to know what she was thinking.

"I wouldn't," he said, keeping his eyes on Bo. "It would be full-time on set."

Morgan stood so abruptly the table shook as she pushed

back. She grabbed up his untouched mug of tea and took it to the sink where she poured it out and dropped the mug in with a clatter. Before Jeff had a chance to say anything, she'd stormed out of the room.

"What was that all about?" Jeff asked his friend, who didn't seem fazed by the outburst.

"I told her before you went to work on set that I didn't think you'd be coming back," Bo said. He tipped his beer up and drained the bottle. "When you came back, she thought I was wrong. Morgan doesn't like the idea of you leaving. I don't know if you've noticed, but she's gotten kind of used to having you around."

Jeff smiled and nodded. The feeling was mutual.

"Anyway," Bo continued. "She was pretty happy to prove me wrong. She said you'd never leave the Lodge, that you loved it here too much. But apparently she was wrong, wasn't she?"

Jeff nodded and then shook his head. "Wait. You didn't think I'd come back?" His leg bounced and he pushed up from the table, unable to sit any longer. "The Lodge is my home."

Bo waited and watched before leaning back in his chair. "No, Jeff. The Lodge is where you work. You can't stay here forever and we both know it."

Jeff walked to the window over the sink that looked out into the forest. He sighed and released a breath. Bo was right. They both knew it, but only one of them was willing to admit it.

"Tell me about the job," Bo said. "And then you can tell me why you haven't accepted it yet."

Jeff and Bo were working on their third beer by the time Jeff finished telling Bo about the job offer. As Jeff knew he would be, Bo was totally onboard with the idea of his buddy trying something new and he couldn't see why Jeff was dragging his feet.

"Take the offer," Bo said for at least the tenth time. "Before they give it to someone else. Hollywood doesn't wait for anybody, especially a horse wrangler. If you don't take the job, you're going to lose it, buddy."

Jeff swirled the bottle around in his hand. "I know it. In fact, I expect Marianne Marshall up here any day to demand a signature on the contract. She's the type of woman who doesn't take no for an answer."

"Then don't say no." Bo pushed up from the table and opened the fridge. "You hungry?" He grabbed some leftover chicken and returned to the table. "Tell me the real reason why you haven't accepted the offer yet."

Jeff snatched a piece of cold chicken and took a bite to keep from answering.

"You don't have to answer me," Bo said. "But it sounds like you're running out of time to figure it out." Bo took a bite of a drumstick at the exact moment the door opened and Morgan returned.

"You're going to ruin your dinner," she admonished him.

"I am? Were you going to make some? Because I certainly wasn't." Bo laughed and pulled Morgan onto his lap. It was a running joke between the two of them that neither of them liked to cook and they had most of their meals up at the Lodge except when Bruno or one of the other chefs brought them something.

"Maybe I was going to heat something up," Morgan teased and bent down to kiss Bo.

Their ease with each other tugged at something inside Jeff. Just as Bo had been before Morgan came along, Jeff had always been happy with playing the field. They'd both had something of a reputation for being ladies' men. Jeff had never given a second thought to having a serious relationship before.

At least not until he'd watched his best friend fall in love. Things changed. And with little Ella looking up to him, his own dating life had taken a serious turn. Somehow when a little girl was paying attention and asking questions, it wasn't so easy to bounce from bed to bed.

Just as Jeff stood to get up and excuse himself, Morgan looked over in his direction. "I'm sorry I got so upset," she said. "I shouldn't have left like that."

He waved away her apology. "It's fine," he said. "It probably came as a bit of a surprise. Besides, I don't even know if I'm going to take it yet."

Morgan slid off Bo's lap and pulled Jeff into a hug. "It wasn't a surprise, Jeff. You can't stay here forever. But knowing that doesn't make it any easier. Ella will be heartbroken to see you go."

Jeff flinched and pulled away. "Can we not tell her yet?" he asked. "At least until it's official. I don't want to upset her for no reason."

Morgan smiled. "You tell her when you're ready," she said.

"Okay, okay," Bo interrupted. "It's not like he's moving to Tibet. It's just a job. Everyone needs to stop making such a big deal about it all."

They all looked at Bo and burst into laughter because he was right.

"And speaking of a job," Jeff said. "I should head over to the Lodge. I had a very interesting visit this morning about a woman who needed a horse for the wedding."

"Andi and Colin's wedding?" Morgan asked. "Andi and I used to work together, that's how I came to work up at the Lodge." She exchanged a glance with Bo, no doubt remembering how they'd met. "You've met her before, haven't you?" She turned back to Jeff.

He nodded. "Of course. Only once or twice though."

"Well, she's just lovely," Morgan continued. "I've missed

her. But I've never seen her so stressed. She came to talk to me about her half-brothers who would be coming. They're twins and total terrors, according to her. It should be fun to find activities for them to do this week." Morgan smiled, because she meant it. She loved nothing more than a challenge when children were concerned.

"Well, I don't think it's just the kids who are the problem," Jeff said. "Her best friend is a piece of work, too."

"Eva?" Morgan gave him a strange look.

"Sounds interesting," Bo said and winked at him.

"Not like that at all," he said, but couldn't help but feel like he was lying to his friends. "She's the exact opposite of my type. The only time I've met a girl more city than Eva was on set. And believe me, I don't need any more of that in my life. Would you believe she came tromping through the snow in tiny little heels and then gave me attitude because she was slipping and sliding and falling in the snow?"

"Unbelievable," Morgan said with a giggle.

Jeff looked between both of his friends, taking in their smiles and knowing looks. "Forget it," Jeff said. "It's not like that at all. You two need to stop thinking of every woman I meet as a potential girlfriend. Especially this one. She's not even remotely my type. Besides, I'm not interested."

"Whatever you say, buddy."

Morgan giggled again and Jeff threw up his arms.

"She's not. Besides, I don't think she's very happy with me. I told her no way was she getting a horse for the wedding, and I get the feeling Eva isn't used to hearing the word no."

"Sounds like a real piece of work," Bo said with a wink.

"Forget it." Jeff threw up his hands in frustration. "I'm outta here. I'll see you both later. Give Ella a hug for me and tell her I still want an ice skating date with her."

He left the cottage and headed out into the crisp afternoon. The sun was quickly disappearing behind the mountains, and it would be dark before too long. He walked quickly, trying to clear his head of everything they'd talked about. But it wasn't the concern over the job that was occupying Jeff's thoughts; it was a certain blond with an attitude he couldn't get clear from his mind.

Chapter Five

DRESSED MUCH MORE SENSIBLY for the weather than she had been the day before, in heavy winter boots she'd borrowed from Carmen, and a down-filled parka she normally reserved for skiing, Eva tugged a knit cap over her ears and headed out into the crisp air for her morning walk.

It was early enough that most of the guests at the Lodge were still sleeping. Wrapped cozily into their beds, snuggling with their loved ones, no doubt. She snorted in disgust at the thought. Even if she did have someone special to keep her warm on a cold winter day, she still wouldn't waste such a beautiful morning by lazing around in bed.

Or would she? An image of Jeff's strong arms wrapped around her, holding her hostage in a toasty bed, occupied her thoughts.

Where did that come from? Eva kicked at the snow on the pathway and stuffed her hands deeper into her parka. She didn't need anybody's arms wrapped around her, especially not that bulky, self-important, horse man's arms. Besides, she had more important things to concern herself with. The last thing she needed was to let Jeff take up room in her mind. Especially with only a few days before the wedding.

Eva picked up her pace and tucked her face further into the collar of her coat. She forced her mind to focus on the details she still needed to take care of. Andi wanted a winter wonderland wedding and Eva knew she'd be able to give it to her. For Andi, anything. But that meant she needed to focus. And the very first thing on her list for the day was centerpieces. In the picture she'd shown Andi, there were pine cones and twigs. It was rustic and beautiful. But it still wasn't right. The concept was too plain; it was missing something.

She scanned the snow-dusted landscape and out to the ridge beyond. It was a stunning view and the green from the pine trees popped against their backdrop of white. If only she could transfer that look indoors. Eva spun slowly, taking in all of her surroundings. A spot of red caught her attention and she stepped forward, leaving the plowed trail to investigate. The snow was deep, but her borrowed boots did the job and soon she was crouching down in front of a fallen log, with a cluster of holly berries growing in a small bush beneath it.

A pop of red. It was perfect. With her phone, Eva snapped a quick picture of the plant before attempting to pick the prickly little sprig.

She should have known better. After all, it wasn't the first time she'd seen holly. But Eva was too excited to use caution and in return was rewarded with the sting of the prickly leaves as it bit into her flesh.

"Ow. Dammit." She put her finger to her mouth and sucked on the cut for a second. When the initial shock subsided, she attempted to pick it again, this time using more caution. Eva was able to snap the little branch and pull away the sprig of berries. She stood from her crouch and admired her find. They were perfect and she could hardly believe she hadn't thought of it before. The berries were exactly what she needed. But she would need a whole lot more than one little sprig to adorn all the centerpieces. Someone would have to know where she could get more. If there was one plant nearby, there was bound to be more.

Re-energized, Eva picked her way through the snow and back to the path. It was next to impossible to run in the clunky boots, but she managed a fast walk and headed straight to the Lodge where she could put together a sample centerpiece to show Andi when they met for breakfast. With any luck, she'd be able to put something together right away so she could get at least one thing crossed off her list.

"I'm not sitting next to your mother and her...her friend," Andi's father said at the same moment Eva came upon the table.

Running late for their breakfast date, it looked as if Andi had found a replacement, but she didn't look happy about it. Eva slid into the seat next to her friend. "Sorry I'm late," she said. "Mr. Williams, it's nice to see you again." Eva smiled her most dazzling smile at him. The one she reserved for problematic clients. Andi shot her a look of gratitude and turned back to her cup of tea.

"Eva," Mr. Williams said. "It's lovely to see you again, dear. But I have to ask, are you in charge of the seating arrangement? Because Andi's telling me it can't be changed and I have to tell you, I'm not sitting next to my ex-wife and her...her partner. It just won't do. How can I explain that to the boys?"

Eva caught the waitress' attention and had her coffee cup filled before calmly answering him. "A wedding is a celebration of love, don't you agree, Mr. Williams?"

He nodded.

"And Bonnie and Val are in love, just as you and Roxanne

are. So my suggestion to you would be, if the boys ask, which I'm not sure they would since five-year-old boys aren't known for their interest in adult relationships, you simply tell them that all of Andi's parents are happy and involved in loving relationships and you all wish that for Andi and Colin as well. But as I said, I doubt very much the question will come up."

Andi flicked a smile in Eva's direction, but both of them remained serious.

"But—"

"Dad," Andi interrupted. "It means a lot that you are all willing to be here for me, and I would love it if I could have all my family sitting together. As you know, it's not a very big place and the wedding is really quite small. It seems silly to have you all spread out in the room."

"And it really would throw everything off as far as the seating arrangements go," Eva chimed in. "I'm sure you agree, Mr. Williams, there are far more important details to take care of for the wedding. Especially with it only being days away." Eva smiled sweetly and stirred some sugar into her coffee.

Andi's dad cleared his throat and took the napkin from his lap. "Yes," he said. "You're both absolutely right. I'm sure the seating arrangement will be fine. As long as it's okay with Bonnie, it will be fine with me."

"I'm sure Mom will be okay with it," Andi said. "But Roxanne?" she asked, getting to the heart of the matter.

"I'll handle Roxanne," he said. "Now, if you'll excuse me. I need to get the boys to the Cub Club. I understand they're going to be doing some snowshoeing or something."

"Sounds fun," Eva lied. "It was nice to see you, Mr. Williams. We'll talk more later about the details of the ceremony."

"Absolutely," he said. "Have fun, girls." And with that he was gone, leaving Eva and Andi alone.

She waited until he was out of sight, but then Andi let out

a deep sigh and said, "Thank you. Honestly, I don't know if I could have handled it so calmly if you hadn't showed up."

"Sorry I was late," Eva said. She took a sip of her coffee. "But he seems okay now. What got him so worked up?"

"It's not him. It's Roxanne," Andi said. She dropped her head into her hands and squeezed her temples. "I swear, if I knew it was going to be so difficult just handling my family all in one place, we would have eloped. This is too much."

The waitress delivered a basket of muffins to the center of the table before leaving them alone. Eva waited and watched her best friend for a moment. Something was wrong. Something more than the stress of the wedding. Andi was a professional and she knew better than anyone how to handle a difficult family when it came to planning an event. Andi never shut down. "Are you okay?" Eva asked her.

Andi nodded, but didn't look up. "Of course I am."

"You're sure? I can't remember the last time I saw you so worked up. I mean, it's just a seating arrangement. We've handled a whole lot worse."

Andi's head shot up and she stared at Eva. "We've never handled my wedding before," she said. "It's different. It's totally different. And now I know what the bride feels like when she loses her mind and starts crying over stupid things like music choices and centerpieces."

"Speaking of centerpieces…"

"We weren't," Andi snapped. Her face crumpled and tears leaked from the corners of her eyes. "I'm sorry, Eva. You don't deserve that. You've been absolutely wonderful. I'm just really on edge right now and I need Colin to wrap up his business meetings and get here already. I'm just feeling really overwhelmed."

Eva reached out and squeezed Andi's hand. "It's okay. Just let me handle things, okay? Maybe we can book you into the spa for a massage while I sort out some details."

Andi nodded. "That sounds good."

It did sound good. Eva made a mental note to book her own massage for the day after the wedding. The way the week was shaping up, she wouldn't have a spare moment to breathe until everything was over. "Good," she said. "I'll get Carmen to book it for you." She reached for a muffin and split it in two.

"And what are you going to do?" Andi asked. "There's still such a big list. I'm sorry, Eva. It's not fair for me to leave everything to you."

Eva waved her protests away. "It's totally fair. If the roles were reversed, you'd do the exact same thing. As for me, I have a plan for the day. I was actually going to tell you that I figured out the perfect addition to the centerpieces this morning. Holly berries. I just need to find someone around here to help me gather enough of them and then I can finish those up. I did a sample one, but I left it in the banquet room, sorry."

"I trust you." Andi swiped at her face with a napkin and took a deep breath. "Holly sounds beautiful," she said. "That's perfect. Why didn't we think of that earlier?"

"I know. That's exactly what I thought." Eva finished her coffee. "But I'll need a whole lot more if I'm going to make it work, and I have no idea where to find them."

"You need Bo," Andi said. "Remember, I told you about him? He's Morgan's new boyfriend."

"I remember." How could she forget? Morgan had left their business Party Hearty, and come to the Lodge, where she, too, had found love. There seemed to be a running theme.

"Anyway," Andi continued, "he's the activity director and he leads the treks into the woods. He'll know exactly where to look. Have you met him yet?"

Eva shook her head and took another bite of a muffin. "The only outdoorsy guy I met was that horse guy you told me to go talk to."

"Jeff?" Andi's face lit up in a smile and she tipped her head to examine Eva.

"That's the guy. I still don't understand why you want a horse. It would be so much easier if you just walked."

"Easier for who?"

Eva tossed the rest of the uneaten muffin on to the plate. "For me obviously." She wouldn't bother telling Andi about the troubles she might have securing a horse for the ceremony. No need to stress her out even more. "Have you even met Jeff? He's a total piece of work and— "

"Hot."

Eva glared at her friend, who, judging by the look on her face, was enjoying Eva's discomfort.

"He's not my type," Eva said.

"But he is hot."

She couldn't deny it. If you could look past his behavior and the whole horse thing, Jeff did have a certain appeal to him. An appeal that she couldn't seem to stop thinking about. Not that she was about to admit it. Not even to Andi.

"He's totally full of himself, and he seems to take a certain pleasure in making me feel like an idiot. And I won't tolerate that in anyone, let alone some guy." Eva crossed her arms and looked away in what she knew was a pout.

"Please don't tell me you fought with him," Andi said.

"Fought with him?" Eva turned back to look at her friend, who had tears glistening in the corner of her eyes again. "I didn't fight with him. Well, unless you call a little stomping, and just a bit of arguing and...okay, I fought with him. But there's no reason to get upset. It was mostly good natured and... Andi, don't cry."

Her friend wiped at her face. "I'm not crying."

Eva knew better than to argue with her.

"I just really can't handle any more fighting. Not with anyone."

"He's the horse guy, Andi. And I promise, it's not fighting fighting. It's more like…" What? Eva thought. Flirting? She pushed the thought from her head. "Anyway, it's not like I'm arguing with your fiancé."

Andi blew her nose and focused on Eva. "I can't handle it with anyone, Eva. Not anyone. Jeff is part of the Lodge and with everything else that's going on…I just don't need one more stress, okay?"

"Andi, it's—"

Eva broke off when Andi started sniffling again.

"I don't know what's gotten into you," she said instead. "I've seen you cry more in the last few days than in the last few years combined. Maybe the stress of the wedding is too much."

"It really is a lot to get all the family together. I knew I should have eloped."

"Stop saying that." Eva reached out and squeezed Andi's arm. "It will be amazing, and I'll take care of everything. Don't worry about a thing."

"And you'll get along with Jeff? Because I really think it would help if you two got along…please."

Isn't that what she was worried about? Getting along with Jeff? If she wasn't careful, she'd want to get along with him too well. She stared into her coffee mug for a few more seconds to be sure her feelings weren't showing on her face. When she looked up, she said, "Fine. I'll do my best."

And just like that, a switch was flipped and Andi broke into a huge smile. "Oh, good," she said. "Because I really thought you might like him."

"Like him, like him? I thought you said I would like Troy?" Eva smiled at the inside knowledge she had on Troy but there was no point telling Andi that right away. "I'm beginning to think you're willing to set me up with any man as long as he has a pulse."

Andi waved away her protests. "Oh, come on," she said. "You know that's not it. Besides, you have to admit, Jeff's hot."

"Who's hot?"

Both women startled at the voice and looked up to find the subject of their discussion looking down on them. Eva flushed what she knew would be an unflattering shade of pink and busied herself with her coffee cup to keep from looking at him.

"You must have some sort of radar," Andi said. "We were just talking about you." Traitor. Eva risked a glance in Andi's direction so she could glare at her, but Andi was ignoring her. Likely on purpose.

"Well, when it comes to pretty ladies, I do try to make it my business to pay attention," Jeff said. He winked in Eva's direction. Coming from anyone else, it would have looked creepy. Eva hated winkers. But there was something about the way Jeff did it that made it look easy and, even if she didn't want to admit it, hot. Her pulse raced, and Eva had to look away to calm her traitorous body.

Eva cleared her throat and tried not to focus on the flutter of desire that Jeff's presence had unwillingly stirred in her. "Don't get too excited, cowboy. I was just telling Andi that you were looking for the perfect horse for her wedding." She stared at Jeff, hoping he'd pick up on her cue. She didn't need Andi worked up again, especially over a horse.

Unaffected by her abruptness, Jeff slid into the empty seat at the table and casually crossed one leg over the other. "About the horse—"

"We'll talk about it later," Eva cut him off and narrowed her eyes at him. Leave it to Jeff to not pick up on her signals.

He gave her a strange look in return and Eva watched as realization finally hit. "As a matter of fact," he said slowly. "I think I may have found a few horses that will work perfectly." He spoke to Andi, but his piercing gaze didn't leave Eva. "I was hoping you would come down to the stables to choose. I usually recommend that you get a feel for the animal before making any big decisions about it."

What the hell did that mean? Did he change his mind about his stupid policy?

"I agree," Eva said, before she could stop herself. "It's like judging someone based on first impressions. Sometimes you need to take a deeper look before making any decisions."

They locked eyes, Eva challenging him to look away first. His gaze didn't waver and it wasn't long before he was the only thing she was focused on. Her breaths deepened, and Jeff was matching her breath for breath. Neither of them would look away.

"What are you two talking about?" Andi interrupted. The spell broken, Eva sat back and fiddled with her coffee cup again.

"Nothing," she mumbled.

"Just that sometimes first impressions aren't the only ones," Jeff said. "Which is why I think Eva should come check out the horses for herself."

"Sounds perfect," Andi said. "I totally trust Eva. And frankly, relaxing is going to be my priority right now. Didn't somebody say something about a massage?"

Jeff laughed. "Sounds good," he said. "I think if a massage was an option for me, I'd gladly take it." He looked directly at Eva when he spoke, and she had to work hard to keep from turning red again.

Men didn't have that type of effect on her. Not ever. She was in charge, in control and never had she let a man get the best of her before.

"Keep dreaming," Eva said.

He opened his mouth to say something, but closed it again.

"But I'm sure Eva can fit that in to her schedule," Andi said.

Both Eva and Jeff swung their heads around to look at Andi.

"Sounds like a great—"

"There's no way—"

They both spoke at once.

Eva shook her head and spoke again before Jeff had a chance. "I can't. I'm way too busy."

"Too busy to come look at a horse or two?" Jeff challenged. "Because I have this policy…"

Damn him and his policy. "Fine," Eva said. "I'll look. But I'm too busy today."

"Really?"

"Actually, yes." Eva straightened up in her chair and tossed her napkin over the mostly uneaten muffin. "I have to go find Bo so he can take me to gather holly for the centerpieces."

Jeff sat back and crossed his arms over his chest. "You won't find him."

"And why not?"

"Bo just took off leading a snowshoe trek into the woods with some kids."

"Oh, that's what the boys were going to do today," Andi said. "It sounds like they do some cool things with the kids club here."

Jeff smiled and easily helped himself to a muffin on the tray. "They do. Morgan and Bo have really—"

"Well, great," Eva interrupted. "I guess I'll have to go find it on my own." She pushed up from the table, needing distance. "I should probably get going."

"Oh no." Jeff abandoned his muffin and stood, blocking her exit. "You can't go out into the mountains on your own. You'll kill yourself."

"I most certainly will not," she said. Eva crossed her arms and glared at him, her chest heaving.

"Right," he said with a grin. "You'd get maybe twenty

minutes out before you froze to death in those little boots and I'd have to come rescue you. Besides, you don't know where to go."

"And you do, I suppose."

"As a matter of fact—"

"Perfect," Andi said. "Jeff, you take her. That way Eva can get everything she needs for the centerpieces."

Eva shot her friend a look, but Andi was already gathering her things. "Eva, don't worry about arranging the massage with Carmen. I'll take care of it. You go and have a good day."

"But, I don't—"

"I'll talk to you later, okay? Bye, Jeff."

Eva considered grabbing her friend and physically stopping her from leaving or at the very least, smacking her upside the head to knock some sense into her, since she was obviously not thinking straight. But in the end, she stood by and watched Andi walk away, leaving her alone with Jeff.

"Well," he said. "Looks like it's just you and me." He offered her his arm. "Shall we?"

After changing back into her parka and boots, Eva met up with Jeff in the main room of the Lodge. She'd used the few minutes alone to calm herself and refocus on the task of collecting holly. She had to stay focused if she was going to get everything finished in time. And she couldn't afford to have Jeff, or anyone for that matter, derail her from that task. Andi was counting on her.

"It looks like you found some reasonable clothes," Jeff said when he saw her.

"I told you when I met you I hadn't planned on having to tromp through the snow."

"I know, I know. I should have shoveled. You told me."

Eva bit back a sharp retort on the tip of her tongue, remembering her promise to Andi. She wouldn't argue with him, even if it was fun. Eva took a deep breath. "Look," she said. "I have a lot to do. Can we get started?"

Jeff held open the door that led out to the courtyard behind the Lodge. "After you, madam."

He really was going to test every one of her nerves. She grabbed her basket and pushed out the door into the cold winter air. Being in such close proximity to Jeff would be challenging, in more ways than one, but she'd been in worse positions before, and handled them with grace. She could certainly handle a man.

"Thank you," Eva said, putting on her sweetest smile.

Jeff let out a low whistle and followed her outside. "Well, you are most certainly welcome, madam. I'm not sure what has caused the shift in your demeanor today, but I like it."

Eva spun around and almost smacked directly into his chest. He was standing so close, she could smell him. A heady mixture of pine, campfire and an earthy maleness that she assumed must come from spending time outside with horses. Involuntarily, she took a deep breath and the heady scent filled her, making her dizzy. She had to take a step back.

Of course, she would have to step on a rock and lose her footing. Jeff reached out and steadied her. "Whoa," he said. "I guess it doesn't matter what type of boot you're wearing. You're just not used to the woods."

Eva yanked her arm away and straightened her coat. "It's not the woods I need to get used to," she said.

"It's me, then." She could tell by the grin on his face he was only joking, but he didn't realize just how close his words hit home. And he didn't need to either.

"You think far too much of yourself," she said. "It's not you I need to get used to. In fact, I could do with a lot less of you."

She turned and started stalking down the path, towards what she hoped was the parking lot.

It was only a moment before he fell into step beside her. "I hope you don't mean that," he said.

"Look." Eva spun and stared at him. "I promised Andi we wouldn't argue."

"But arguing with you is fun."

She tipped her head. "Look, I mean it, okay? I promised her and—"

The cocky smile fell from his face and he pursed his lips together. "Okay," he said. "I didn't realize I was making it so difficult."

"Well, you are." Eva dropped the edge from her voice and when she saw the hurt look in his eyes, she tried to smile. "But this should be fun," she lied. "I've never been out in the woods in the winter." Or really, any time, she stopped herself from adding.

The light in his eyes returned when he said, "You'll love it. There's nothing more beautiful than snow-covered pines and the stillness of the forest. You really can't understand until you experience it for yourself, but there's nothing else like it."

"I'm sure it's magical." Eva smiled and surprised herself that she didn't even have to force herself to sound genuine.

"You'll love the peacefulness," Jeff said. "Just step right up."

Eva started when she saw where Jeff had led her. They'd gone past the Lodge utility Jeep and were stopped in front of a sleigh. A sleigh with a horse attached to it.

Instinctively, Eva took a step back. "Oh no."

"No to the horse? Or the sleigh?" Jeff took her arm to keep her from running, which she probably would have if he wasn't holding on.

"Both," she said. "There's no way. I told you, I don't like horses."

"But I'm not asking you to ride one," he said. He slowly

moved her towards the animal. "I'm asking you to sit in a sleigh. Surely you can't be opposed to that?"

She shook her head, but realized how stupid she would sound if she objected to something so benign as a sleigh ride. After all, she reasoned with herself, there's an entire Christmas jingle dedicated to sleigh rides. Besides, if she couldn't even handle a sleigh ride, he'd never agree to giving Andi a horse for the wedding. "Okay," she said, still shaking her head. "How bad could it be?"

Jeff's face lit up with the smile she was beginning to get used to, and he hopped up into the sleigh with one big step. He extended his hand to her and against her better judgment, she accepted, letting his big, warm hand envelope hers and pull her aboard.

Chapter Six

HE TRIED NOT to notice how cute she was, but every time Eva made a squeal or squeezed her hands around the railing of the sleigh, Jeff noticed. Oh, did he notice. It was refreshing to see this hard-edged woman, who always had a quick retort, let down her guard. Even if it was only for a few seconds at a time.

He barely needed to guide Clover down the snowy track, but he kept a loose grip on the reins just in case she spooked, and also to show Eva he was totally in control of the horse and there really was nothing to be concerned about. "See," he said, after a few moments. "I told you there was nothing to worry about. Horses are absolutely safe. In fact, horses and humans go together like—"

"The ride isn't over yet," she interrupted. "There's still plenty of time for something to go wrong." Eva squeezed her eyes shut and tucked her face down into the collar of her parka. "How much farther?"

Jeff didn't even try to hide his smile. Instead, he carefully lifted her left hand from the death grip it had on the rail and squeezed it in his own. "Look around," he said gently. "It's beautiful out here. I promise Clover knows what she's doing and you'll hate yourself if you miss the amazing scenery."

She didn't immediately pull her hand away, which Jeff took as a small victory. His first impression of Eva had been wrong. The more time he spent with her, the more he was beginning to think there was more to her and the crusty tough girl act was just that, an act.

"Honestly," he said, when she didn't open her eyes right away. "It's totally safe. I swear."

First one eye opened, and then the other, and Eva lifted her head and looked at him. "You swear?"

"Scouts' honor." Jeff let go of her hand to hold up two fingers in a Scouts promise, and then instantly regretted losing the contact.

Eva slowly looked around. "It is pretty," she said.

Jeff followed her gaze and took in the snow-dusted pines, the blue sky overhead and the track ahead. "I think it's the most magical time of year in the woods," he said. His voice was only slightly more than a whisper. It happened every time he went deep into the forest; a sense of peace overtook him and it didn't take long before he felt completely calm and relaxed. It was the only place he could still his thoughts long enough to really think. And he was willing to leave it for a job in show business? The thought of his impending decision slammed into him. How could he leave? It was a great opportunity, but for what?

A blur of motion out of the corner of his eye grabbed his attention at the same time Clover noticed. A deer, and Clover snorted and flipped her head in greeting to the wild animal.

"What was that?" Eva gripped Jeff's leg and shrunk down next to him.

"Just a deer." He secretly smiled at the contact. "Clover was just saying hi. Nothing to get worked up about," he said.

"Maybe you should tell the horse that," Eva said. "You

shouldn't snort when you're saying hi." A bit of the edge he'd experienced with her earlier had snuck back into her voice, but when he glanced down to look at her, her eyes were sparkling with humor. She'd obviously relaxed enough to trust him, at least for the moment. And Jeff couldn't be sure if it was that acknowledgment, or that she still had a grip on his thigh, that was causing his mind to run wild. Whatever it was, he was definitely enjoying himself.

They sat in quiet for a few more moments, and eventually Eva pulled away from Jeff's leg but let her left hand rest on the bench between them, and he fought the urge to take it in his own again.

"So, about the horse," Eva said, and it took a moment for Jeff to realize what horse exactly she was talking about. "Did you mean what you said at breakfast? Andi can have the horse for the wedding?"

Jeff pretended to think about it some more. "Well," he said. "I have my reservations. But, I think so."

Her face lit up in a radiant smile. God, she was gorgeous. "You'll still need to come and pick one out, though," he added, knowing it would mean spending more time with her.

The smile fell off her face as she no doubt contemplated the options. Finally, she nodded. "If I have to. But you have to understand, I really don't like horses. And they don't like me."

"Well, that's just crazy." Jeff snuck his hand closer to hers. "Horses are the most gentle creatures around. What possibly could have happened to make you hate them?"

Eva stared at him, seriousness in her eyes. "The last time I rode one, it bucked me off and broke my arm. They hate me."

He did his best not to laugh. "Let me guess, you were a kid at camp?"

"How did you know?"

"It's a pretty common story," he said, unable to keep the laughter from his voice.

Eva tried to look mad, but her smile gave her away. "Well, common or not, I still don't trust them."

"Fair enough." Jeff closed the gap, and wrapped his fingers over her hand. "Trust is something you have to build." His words were loaded with meaning, but he didn't want to push. "Look at Clover here," he said. "You're doing a pretty good job trusting her."

She didn't move her hand, so Jeff gave it a squeeze, and she smiled. "I guess I am," she said. "Maybe there's hope for me yet."

They fell into silence again and Jeff snuck a look at Eva, who seemed to be taking in the passing trees, searching the woods for something. Maybe she, too, felt the calming feeling of the forest? Maybe, just like him, she was seeking answers in the trees, too?

"So, am I looking for large bushes of holly, or will they be in little bunches?" she asked, breaking the tranquility.

Of course. Jeff could have smacked himself. She was searching for centerpiece material. Not answers or anything deeper than decorations. He shook his head, clearing it of the thoughts that had sprung up so unexpectedly, and mostly unwelcome. Eva wasn't his type, and it would serve him well to remember that.

"Just a little farther, and there's a spot that has quite a big cluster of holly sprigs. I don't know how much you're looking for, but it should be enough to do a few arrangements, I'd imagine." He didn't look at her when he spoke, but kept his eyes trained on the path ahead.

Jeff could feel her gaze on him when she said, "Thank you." Her voice was soft and not for the first time, she caught him off guard.

"You don't have to—"

"No. I do. I never would have been able to find my way out here by myself. And I know—oh, is that some?"

Jeff spun around, his mind racing to keep up with what she was saying. He'd barely pulled Clover to a stop before Eva hopped out of the sleigh and picked her way through the snowbank to where she'd spotted some holly.

"Looks like you found it," he said, mostly to himself.

"Can you bring me my basket?" she called to him and like a dutiful subject, he gathered her things and went to join her.

Eva could hardly believe how excited she got just spotting the coveted plant. And thank goodness she'd seen it when she had, because she might have actually told Jeff how sorry she was for being rough on him and how much she was actually enjoying her time with him. And she was. Spending a bit of time with him made her realize that her promise to Andi wasn't going to be hard to keep. But even if she thought it, she couldn't say it. And she most certainly couldn't act on it. Even if her body was betraying her with an intense attraction to him. No, it was definitely a good thing that she'd spotted the holly when she had.

"Here you go," he said, coming up behind her and handing her the clippers. "If you cut it off low enough, you should have a decent amount for an arrangement without hurting the plant."

"Oh. I hadn't thought of that," she said and instantly felt ashamed. Of course she should have thought about killing the plants. It wouldn't do to sacrifice a forest full of holly plants for the sake of a few wedding table arrangements.

"It's fine," Jeff said. "I really don't think you're going to kill them. I wouldn't worry too much about it. They're pretty hardy." He reached out and took the clippers from her. "How much do you need?"

"Just a few sprigs of berries for each centerpiece, and I

think we'll have fifteen tables, plus the gift table and the head table and—"

"So quite a bit?" Jeff laughed and started clipping.

"I guess more than I thought."

"Well, start looking around because this plant isn't going to give you what you need."

Eva started and for a moment, she could have sworn he'd said that he wasn't going to give her what she needed. But that would be ridiculous. All they'd done since they'd met was argue; why would he even be thinking of her in any other light? Except there had been that moment on the sleigh... Eva let her mind wander and remember the feel of his hand in hers, and then later, the strong muscles of his leg as she'd gripped onto him. He'd made her feel safe, and when was the last time any man had done that for her?

"Eva?"

She shook her head and focused.

Jeff looked at her and raised an eyebrow. "You okay?"

"Of course." She nodded. "I'm fine. I was just trying to figure out how much more I would need."

He gave her a look that told her without any uncertainty that he didn't believe a word she said.

"Are you sure that's all you're thinking about?" He took a step towards her, closing the gap. His voice was low, his gaze intense, as he said, "Because it looks like you're thinking about a whole lot more." He reached out and tucked a hair behind her ear. Reflexively, she closed her eyes and when his lips met hers, she wasn't nearly as shocked as she should have been.

Eva melted into him, her body responding instantly to Jeff's kiss. With one hand, he pulled her into him; his other hand cupped her cheek, holding her close.

His lips moved against hers, softly searching but not demanding. She responded in kind, electricity buzzing through her in an intensity that surprised her. She let out a small moan, and pulled away, common sense crashing into her. "I don't…I think…" Eva couldn't finish the thought. Her mind was spinning; her body pulsing.

"Eva, I…"

She stepped back and Jeff reached for her in the same instant but she dodged him. Her response to him was too intense. Too strong. She needed a moment to think and clear her head. Eva turned so her back was facing him, took a deep breath and opened her eyes.

"Can we—"

"It looks like there's a bunch more over there behind that pile of logs," she said, interrupting him.

"Great."

Welcoming the opportunity to put some space between them, Eva grabbed her basket and immediately charged through the snow in the direction of the holly.

"Wait," he said. "I'll come with you. It might be slippery over there on the logs."

"I'll be fine."

"I just don't want—"

She turned around. "You don't want what?" She held his gaze, unsure of what she really wanted his answer to be.

"I don't want you to get hurt," he said after a moment.

"Well, that makes two of us." No longer sure what they were talking about, Eva pulled her gaze away from his and took a confident step onto a snow-covered log. Her foot slipped a bit. She bit her bottom lip, but maintained her balance.

"Eva," Jeff said behind her. "Really, be careful in the logs."

She took another step. "I'm fine," she said as she took a big step up onto another log. As soon as the words left her mouth and her boot made contact with the wood, she felt her foot slipping. She tried to right herself by stepping up with her other foot, but that only served to throw her off-balance further, and the only thing that went through her mind as she crashed through the logs was how infuriating it was that Jeff was right.

Moments later that thought flew out of her head too, replaced by piercing sensations of pain shooting up her arm.

"Eva!" She vaguely heard Jeff's voice call out but it seemed so far away, like an echo. Eva thought she might have heard him talking to her, his voice a mumble in the back of her head. The blue mid-day sky grew darker and after a moment, the sun was all but gone, and there was nothing but darkness.

Jeff scrambled over the logs as fast as he could in the snow. Eva had gone down hard.

"Eva?" He called her name again, but still no answer. Just his luck that she'd pass out in the woods, and after he'd worked so hard to convince her there was no danger. Of course, that had been with horses and technically...

"Eva," he said again as he reached her side. He tugged off his knit cap and gently lifted her head so he could slide it underneath. "Hey," he said. "Are you okay?" His eyes scanned down her body, coming to rest on her arm that was twisted and wedged between two logs.

She fluttered her eyes, gradually coming to, so he spoke again. "You're okay." He kept his voice soft and neutral. "You must have blacked out for a moment."

Eva blinked again and slowly her beautiful eyes started to focus on him. "It...it hurts." Her voice was barely a whisper, but he could hear the pain laced through her words.

"Don't try to move your arm," he said. "Let me check it out first."

"It hurts. I just need to—" She pulled and a look of pain and panic flashed across her face.

"Oh, no, you don't," Jeff said. He gently pressed her

back down, holding his hand on her shoulder. "I don't want you to cause more damage. Let me look at it." He held her gaze, trying to convey with his eyes that she'd be okay. It must have worked because she nodded once and closed her eyes against the pain she knew must be coming.

Jeff rested his hand on her shoulder for a moment more before wiping the stray tear off her cheek. Eva's breaths were coming quick and shallow and he knew he didn't have long before she'd try to get up again. Reluctantly, he pulled his gaze away and got to work.

Fortunately, the logs hadn't shifted terribly in the fall, and Eva simply had the misfortune of slipping directly between two of them. Jeff lifted the top one away, to expose her arm. "Okay," he said. "Just slide it out, but don't try to bend it yet. It might be broken."

Eva did as she was told and soon was free, cradling her left arm to her chest.

"Are you okay?" He slid off the log pile and came around, so he was standing on the ground next to Eva, who was still somewhat precariously balanced on the logs.

"Does it look like I'm okay?" she snapped and regret instantly crossed her face. "I'm sorry," she said. "It's not totally your fault."

"Not totally?" He crossed his arms in front of him and examined her.

She shot him a look but didn't say anything further. Even when she was in pain, the woman couldn't cut him a break.

But they couldn't stay in the woods all day. It would be getting dark eventually, and if she sat too much longer, she'd be soaked and then frozen, and the last thing he needed was to hear about that. Jeff sighed. "We should get you back to the Lodge," he said. "Let me help you up."

She scooted towards the edge of the log pile as best she

could with only one arm. She winced with the movement and bit her lower lip. "I can manage."

He had no doubt that she could manage on her own, but it would probably mean hurting herself further and there was no way he was going to stand by and watch that. Besides that, there was nothing he wanted more than to have her body pressed up against his. He crossed the space between them and slid one arm under her legs, lifting her.

"Hey. You don't have to—" She swatted at him and tried to wiggle away.

"Cut it out, Eva. You're going to hurt yourself." He pulled her close and wrapped his other arm around her shoulders, pressing her to his chest. Aware of her sore arm, he had her pinned, and easily cradled in his arms.

"Put me down." She tried to squirm, but didn't get anywhere. "I don't need you to treat me like a child."

"Well, if you're going to act like one…"

"I am not—"

"Seriously," he said, forcing the humor out of his voice. "Just relax. Your arm might be broken and the last thing you need is to slip and fall again. It won't kill you to let me help you."

She stilled in his arms and he could practically feel her entire body sulking. "Fine," she said.

Jeff picked his way carefully through the snow, which was considerably harder with Eva in his arms, and deposited her gently into the sleigh.

"You're welcome," he said with a smile.

Eva huffed and looked away. "I didn't ask for your help."

"Well, you're still very welcome." He couldn't help it but his smile grew wider. There was something about Eva that fired him up and he loved watching the way her skin flushed when she got angry.

Leaving her in the sleigh, Jeff returned to the log pile and retrieved Eva's basket and cutters. He scooped up the bits of holly that had fallen out and delivered them to her before sliding into the seat next to her.

"What do you think you're doing?" she asked him.

"Is this a trick question?" He peered over at her and took in her pout mixed with a grimace of pain that diluted the effect she was no doubt going for. Jeff pointed to her arm, which was starting to swell. "I'm taking you back to the Lodge," he said with more seriousness. "That arm does not look good and we need to get it looked at properly."

"I'm fine." Eva attempted to cross her arms but a groan of pain escaped her lips. "Okay," she admitted. "It hurts. But I really need the holly. I don't have any more time and I need to get the centerpieces done. Andi is counting on me."

"I think she'd understand."

Eva shook her head. "No. I mean, yes. Of course she'd understand. But I promised my best friend an amazing wedding that she didn't have to lift a finger to create and I intend to deliver on that promise. I need the holly. Just give me a few more minutes to—"

"Oh no," he said. "There's no way you're going back out there. Since I've met you, all you've done is slip and fall in the snow and I will not be responsible for any further injuries. No way."

"Jeff. I need the holly."

She genuinely looked upset and no matter what, Jeff didn't want to see her unhappy. He resisted the urge to kiss her frown away, but instead he sighed and stood up, grabbing the basket and clippers as he did so. "I'll do it."

"You don't have to."

"Yes. I do." He glanced down at Eva, who looked much smaller and fragile than she had earlier, and softened his tone. "It's not a big deal. It will only take me a minute. Will you be warm enough?"

A tiny smile played across her lips and he hoped she'd say no, so he could warm her up himself. But she nodded and said, "Yes. Thank you, Jeff."

"You can thank me later," he said and held her gaze just long enough to convey what he hoped was an invitation for another kiss, before he headed off through the snow to fill her basket with holly and ultimately see that sweet smile again.

Chapter Seven

EVA POPPED two more painkillers in her mouth and grabbed her bottle of water with her good hand. Her arm hurt way more than she cared to admit, especially to Jeff, but she was thankful he'd pushed the issue of getting her back to the Lodge and to the doctor.

She'd been reassured it wasn't broken, just a bad sprain, which in her mind might as well have meant it was broken because she sure couldn't do much with her left arm all bandaged up and in a sling. But the doctor insisted it would feel better in a few days, and with any luck she'd be fine for the actual wedding.

The pills might help with the swelling, but they still weren't going to get her centerpieces done. Eva stared at the pile of materials in front of her. Jeff had done a fabulous job collecting holly for her and really, he'd managed to find more in five minutes than she probably could have gathered all after-noon. But now, with only one good hand, it was going to take three times as long to put everything together.

Eva took another swallow of water before putting her bottle to the side and pulling a glass bowl towards her. She took two big sprigs of pine and wedged them as best she could into the bowl. Next, she grabbed a birch branch and tried to artfully place it between the pine boughs.

"Not bad," she said, taking a step back to examine her work. "I can do this."

She reached into her basket for a sprig of holly.

"Ouch. Dammit." A prickly leaf bit into her finger and she stuck the sore finger in her mouth.

"Well, it looks like someone isn't having a very lucky day."

Eva spun at the voice and couldn't help but smile when she saw Troy lounging against the doorjamb. "I've had better days," she said.

Troy pushed away and sauntered into the room. His blond hair was perfectly brushed, and his crisp buttoned-down shirt was tucked neatly into his dark denim jeans, making him look every bit the city boy in the woods.

"What happened, darling?" Troy grimaced when he saw Eva's bandaged arm. "Looks like more than holly got you there."

"Would you believe it was holly related?"

He laughed and took the sprig from her hands. "Well, if it was the holly, I think it's my duty as your fake date to help you sort it out. Let me help."

"What do you know about wedding centerpieces?" she asked. "I mean, no offense."

"None taken, darling. But as it happens, I do know a thing or two." He leaned in and whispered in Eva's ear. "Don't tell my business associates, but I have a secret passion for decorating and parties, and when you put them together...well, it's kind of a hobby of mine."

"You don't say?"

"I didn't." He winked at her and tucked the holly into the pines, in just the way Eva would have done it herself. She nodded her head approvingly.

"I told you I had skills," he said.

"I never would have guessed. But since you're here…" Eva waved her arm over the stack of empty glass vases waiting to be filled.

"There's nothing I'd enjoy more," Troy said, and leaned in to kiss her on the cheek. "After all, that's what I'm here for."

She smiled and reached up with her good hand to pat his cheek. "If only you were straight," she said. "Then you'd be perfect."

After dropping Eva off at the Lodge and seeing Clover back to the stable, Jeff had been anxious to get back and see how Eva was doing. It didn't look like her wrist was broken, but it was definitely sprained and the last thing he wanted was to see that look of pain on her face again.

Besides, maybe there was something more he could do to help. After trudging through the snow to gather her holly, she'd been much happier, despite the sore arm, and he'd even made her smile a few more times. He didn't want to admit it, not even to himself, but Eva was a force and the more time he spent with her, the more he realized that she was a force he'd like to reckon with.

Jeff slipped through the main doors of the Lodge and ran straight into Carmen. He usually welcomed the opportunity to stop and catch up with the friendly, overworked woman who was single-handedly in charge of guest relations at the Lodge. But it wasn't a usual day.

"Oh, Jeff. I'm glad I caught you."

He stopped and gave her his biggest smile. "It's always nice to see you, too," he said. "But I really can't chat right now."

"Don't I know that feeling?" She gestured to her clipboard, which no doubt held a to-do list a mile long. "But there was a message for you earlier. I was going to leave it in your mailbox, and then I realized you never check your mailbox." She shot him a look. "So anyway, here you go." She thrust a folded-up piece of paper at him.

He stuck it in his pocket without reading it. "Thanks," he mumbled.

"Aren't you going to even look at it? The lady on the phone said it was important."

Oh, he was sure it was important. His stomach twisted in a knot and glanced over Carmen's shoulder. "Nah," he said. "I know what it says."

There was no doubt that it was Marianne Marshall. She still wanted an answer and he knew he'd have to give it. The thing was, if she'd called yesterday, he'd been almost sure of his answer. But after spending the afternoon in the woods with his favorite horse…and a beautiful woman…the last part popped into his head. He shook it away. At any rate, he still couldn't be certain that leaving the Lodge was what he wanted. But he knew he better figure it out quick.

"Jeff?" Carmen was waving her hand in front of his face. "Earth to Jeff."

He blinked hard, his friend coming back into focus in front of him. "Sorry," he said. "I was just thinking about something."

"Or someone?"

"What?" Jeff shook his head in protest. "No. Why would you think that it had anything to do with a woman?"

Carmen gave him a sly smile. "I didn't say it was a woman you were thinking about. But you did."

She laughed but Jeff didn't join in. Instead, thoughts he didn't want to consider tumbled through his brain. He should be focusing on his career, his future. But instead he couldn't get Eva out of his head. Maybe that was a reason right there to consider leaving the Lodge? He mulled over the thought. After all, Eva lived in the city. He would be living in the city. It was next to impossible to find and have a long-term relationship with anyone at the Lodge. But if he moved...

No, he would not, could not, let a woman or even the thought of a woman influence his decision. Never in his life had he made any decision based on a woman, let alone one who liked to push his buttons, and test him at every move. Except for when they were kissing. The thought slammed into him and sent his mind reeling in a whole new direction. Kissing Eva had been intense, that was for sure. He never would have thought that someone who was as uptight as she was would be capable of expressing that much heat in a simple kiss. But it didn't matter how hot the kiss was; it had nothing to do with his future. Nothing.

"It was a slip of the tongue," he said to Carmen after a moment. He patted his pocket where he'd tucked the message. "I'll call her back soon."

Carmen squeezed his arm, before slipping past him. "Whatever you think, Jeff." She moved to leave, but something stopped her. "Oh, Jeff. I heard Andi wanted a horse for the wedding."

He nodded. "She does, but you know how I feel about that."

"I do," Carmen said. "But it's Andi and Colin."

Jeff smiled. He'd already come to the same conclusion; of course he was going to let them have a horse. But it wouldn't hurt to keep Eva guessing a little longer. "Don't worry, Carmen. I'll make it happen."

"Oh, I'm not worried. You always do the right thing, Jeff."

Jeff watched her walk away and let her words sink in.

He definitely didn't always do the right thing. But it was time to see what he should do.

With a final look behind him, and a deep breath, Jeff headed down the hall to the banquet room in search of Eva. At the very least, he could start by doing the right thing when it came to helping her out, especially with a sore arm. Lord knows she was in over her head with this wedding and Jeff was pretty sure he could find something he could help with. Besides, maybe he'd be rewarded with that sweet smile of hers.

Jeff grabbed the handles of the heavy wood banquet room doors and started to pull them open when the sound of female laughter floated across the air. Was it Eva's laughter? He couldn't be sure since he'd never had the pleasure of making her laugh, but something deep inside him instinctually knew it was her.

The sound made his breath catch in his throat as if he were a teenager in love and instead of shaking away the feeling the way he might have in the past, Jeff embraced it. So what if he liked being with her? She challenged him and sparked something in him in a way no other woman had. At least, none that he could remember. And that was something worth exploring. Especially if it meant kissing her again.

With a wide smile on his face, Jeff again started to push open the doors but this time he stopped short when he heard a man's voice. It sounded friendly. Teasing, flirting. Eva laughed again.

Bracing himself for something he knew he wouldn't want to see, Jeff pushed the door open only enough to peer into the room. He was right. He didn't want to see it. A tall blond and very neatly dressed man was standing so close to Eva, he had to be violating her personal space. Jeff expected her to lash out, tell him to back up the way she might do if it was him standing so close. But she didn't. Instead, when the man tucked a piece of hair behind her ear and whispered something in her ear, Eva laughed again. That beautiful, carefree sound that hit him straight in the gut. Only now, knowing it was another man eliciting the sound he'd been craving to hear, it didn't sound quite so amazing.

Jeff glanced down at his own clothes. Worn jeans, a t-shirt

that had been washed more times than was probably reasonable, his favorite denim work jacket and a dirty pair of cowboy boots. He couldn't compete with the slick man standing next to Eva. A man who was probably much more her type.

After all, hadn't she told him earlier that she'd promised Andi she wouldn't argue with him? Is that what the kiss was about? Simply being nice to him? No. He shook his head. It was more than that. He looked again at Eva and the man who was far too friendly to simply be a friend. But maybe it wasn't? He thought. Maybe he'd read way more into the situation than there was.

"Dumb ass," Jeff muttered. He turned to leave, but in doing so, managed to bump into the doorjamb making enough racket that Eva and her boyfriend both turned in his direction.

"Dammit," he said, and then he turned and managed the biggest smile he could that he hope didn't look too forced.

The second she saw Jeff standing in the door, a flash of guilt that didn't make sense flooded through her, and she knew her face probably showed it clearly. But guilt for what? She took two steps away from Troy and instinctively moved towards the door. And Jeff.

"Jeff," she said. "Were you looking for me?" What a dumb question, she silently reprimanded herself. Why should she assume he'd be looking for her? It's not like one kiss meant they were together, or even friends really.

"I was just…" His eyes darted around the room, refusing to meet her gaze. "I was…well, I was wondering how your arm was." Jeff finally gestured to her bandaged wrist. "How is it? Are you okay?"

Eva pulled her arm close and smiled at his concern. It was sweet that he cared, and she couldn't help but be touched. "It's fine," she said. "Just a sprain, which is good. Except it does make it a little hard to get things done."

"Which is where I come in." Troy stepped up, closing the distance between them. He put his arm around Eva and careful of her sore wrist, pulled her close. "I'm Troy," he said. He held out his right hand to Jeff and after a moment, Jeff came farther into the room and took it.

"I didn't know you had a…a—"

"Troy is a friend," Eva said, quickly. She could feel Troy looking at her strangely, no doubt remembering their earlier discussion and agreement for him to be her fake date. Looking at Jeff, it suddenly didn't seem like such a good idea anymore.

"A really, really good friend," Troy said. He gave her a squeeze and kissed her on the cheek. "Isn't that right, darling?"

Instead of answering right away, Eva watched Jeff. She knew she hadn't imagined their connection earlier. Especially when he'd kissed her. There was a spark between them she'd never felt before. But even without it, things had shifted when they were out in the woods. She'd felt it. Eva focused on Jeff, willing him to give her some sort of sign that he'd felt it too.

Jeff planted his feet and crossed his arms over his muscular chest, his jaw set. He raised an eyebrow and the cool, detached man she'd met at the stables that first day was back. Maybe she'd been wrong.

Troy squeezed her again and she looked up into his eyes full of questions. She knew she was being flaky. She'd asked him to help her out and now she was set to change her mind and make him look like an idiot. That wasn't fair. Besides that, no matter how much she was attracted to Jeff, it wouldn't work. He was a rough around the edges mountain man. He worked with horses, for goodness' sake. And hadn't she had her fair share of failed relationships already? No, it would be easier if she ignored whatever had happened in the woods, and made it through the wedding, and her time at the Lodge, with Troy.

Eva slowly exhaled and purposely looking away from Jeff, she said to Troy, "That's right, sweetie."

She knew if she looked at him, Jeff would be able to see the uncertainty in her eyes. But worse than that, she couldn't bear to see if she'd hurt him. The kiss they'd shared had been real enough to her if her body's reaction was any indication, and she'd been around long enough to know he'd felt something, too. But maybe he was just that kind of guy, she thought, her eyes still averted. Maybe taking women out to the woods and kissing them was just a regular day for him? Maybe Jeff didn't care at all.

She had to know.

Before she chickened out, Eva swung her head around, letting her hair whip across her face, and stared directly at Jeff. His handsome face was impossible to read. At first glance, it looked like a mask of indifference locked onto his features. But there was something else too. Hurt? Or did she just want it to be something more?

"Jeff, I want to—"

He held up his hand to quiet her. "I'll leave you alone. I was just wondering how your arm was," he said. "That's all."

Indifference, Eva thought. It was definitely indifference Jeff was feeling. The casual way he was brushing her off was all the evidence she needed.

"It's going to be fine," Eva said. "Thank you for all your help." She looked down because it was so much easier than looking at his handsome face. "I really mean it. I don't know what I would have done if you—"

"It looks like you're in good hands now," Jeff interrupted with a gruffness she couldn't ignore.

Eva looked up. His mouth was pressed into a firm line and he spoke through gritted teeth. He did care. The thought crashed through Eva's consciousness. He wouldn't be angry if he didn't feel something. But what?

"I'll leave you to it," Jeff said.

He turned to leave and it took everything Eva had in her to hold herself back from stopping him. Jeff pulled the door open and moments before he strode through it, Eva called out, "Jeff."

He froze but didn't turn around. Eva could see his muscles in his strong back tensing under his t-shirt, waiting for whatever she was going to say next. The thing was, she didn't know. She just knew she needed to stop him. Heat and confusion flowed through her, muffled by the throbbing of her arm. Her arm. That was it.

"Will you let me buy you dinner tonight as a thank-you?"

Troy squeezed her shoulder and she looked up to the question in his eyes. Damn.

"I mean, will you let us buy you dinner?" she corrected. Troy smiled and shook his head. She didn't even want to know what he thought of the scene playing out in front of him, but she could only imagine.

With his hand still on the door, Jeff turned around and for a minute, Eva was certain he was going to refuse. Instead, a slow smile played on his lips. He crossed his arms over his chest and nodded. "Okay," he said.

Aware of Troy with his arm still protectively wrapped around her, Eva swallowed her smile and said, "Good. Six o'clock then at the Grill? It's just down past the lobby, by the—"

"I know where it is."

"Of course you do," she said. "So, I'll see you...I mean, we'll see you then."

Jeff's eyes focused like beams into her soul, stirring emotions she wasn't sure she still possessed. But despite the intensity, she couldn't look away.

"I'm already looking forward to it," he said. And just when

Eva didn't think she'd be able to stand the tension in the air for one second longer, he turned and left.

She slumped forward as if he'd taken all the air out of the room with him. Fortunately, Troy, who still had a grip on her, caught her and guided her to a chair before she could fall over. He chuckled and brushed a stray hair away from her eyes. "Something funny?" She looked up into his face, full of humor.

"I've just never seen two people work so hard to pretend they're not interested in each other, is all." Troy left her sitting in the chair and moved back to the table full of centerpieces.

"I'm not interested in him," Eva protested, but even as she did, she could taste the bitterness of the lie. "It's not worth it, anyway. Besides, I accepted you as my fake date. It wouldn't be fair to renege on that arrangement."

"Oh, darling. I promise you I wouldn't hold it against you if you tossed me aside for Mr. Cowboy. I would absolutely understand."

Eva narrowed her eyes at him. "Don't tell me—"

"He's not my type," Troy said with a grin. "But he's yours."

She crossed her arms and a moment too late realized her mistake. "Ouch. Stupid wrist." Eva cradled her wrist in her lap. "He's not my type either," she said as defiantly as she could manage. "I don't go for the rough, outdoorsy guys. I like a smooth, clean-cut business man all the way."

"Like myself?" Troy pointed at himself with a sprig of pine and she couldn't help but laugh.

"Yes, just like you," she said. "But I prefer that the men I date like women."

He tossed the pine to the table. "Details, details. So," Troy said, changing the subject. "What exactly was your plan for dinner tonight? Should we stage a dramatic breakup in the restaurant? That would get people talking."

That would also get Andi stressed out, Eva thought. The last thing Andi needed was more drama of any kind. Even if it was totally fake. She pushed up from the chair and made her way to the table where she fingered the pinecones. What exactly was her plan?

"Or," Troy continued, "you could tell Mr. Cowboy that we have an open relationship and I'm totally okay with you dating him."

"Troy!" Eva tossed a pinecone at him, which he dodged artfully. "Are you out of your mind?"

He shrugged and went back to creating centerpieces. "It was just a thought."

Eva walked around the room, slowly taking in the arrangement of the tables, the cloth Troy had draped along the walls, and the twinkling lights and snowflakes that were hung from the ceiling. There was still so much to do. She didn't have time to be worrying about a guy. Her eyes landed on a piece of holly that had fallen to the ground. She bent to pick it up and smoothed her fingers along the glossy leaves. It didn't matter if she didn't have time, and that he wasn't her type. She couldn't get him out of her head.

"I have a plan," she said to Troy.

Chapter Eight

IT HAD SEEMED like a good idea at the time, Eva thought. These types of things always did. But as she waited at the table for Jeff, she couldn't help but have second thoughts about her plans. Troy had agreed to grab something to eat at the pub so she could be alone with Jeff and come clean to him about her fake date with Troy. She'd had enough deception in her relationships, and although whatever was happening with Jeff was far from a relationship, she was tired of playing games.

Troy seemed to be fairly satisfied with eating alone in the pub, and Eva promised to text him later to fill him in on everything that happened with Jeff. Secretly, she hoped it would be much later. But if he didn't show up soon, her report to Troy would turn out a whole lot differently than she wanted it to.

She looked down to her blue tank dress, which she hoped wasn't too dressy for the occasion. It was the only thing she could find that would accommodate her bandaged arm and the sling. She'd done her best to get ready by herself, brushing her hair and trying to apply makeup, but in the end she'd opted for a more natural look than she usually wore, only because putting on eyeliner and mascara with one hand was quite a bit trickier than she ever would have thought.

"Excuse me," she said to a passing waiter. "Could you tell me what time it is?" She could have checked her phone, and despite the fact that she'd asked the waiter twice already, she needed confirmation of what she already knew.

"It's 6:35," the waiter said. He gave her a knowing look, no doubt because he assumed she'd been stood up.

But that's exactly what had happened, wasn't it? She must have really misread the signs Jeff had been throwing out. And she never misread signs from men. Never. Except…

"Thank you," Eva told the waiter, absentmindedly looking up. She took a sip of her water and focused on the empty seat in front of her. Almost forty minutes. It was official—she'd been stood up.

Before she got up to leave, she looked around one last time still unable to process that he didn't come.

"It's probably for the best," she said to herself.

"It usually is."

Eva spun around and couldn't help but smile at the waiter, who was far more perceptive than she'd given him credit for.

"It's his loss," the waiter said. "If he stood you up," he looked her up and down appreciatively, "he's not worth it."

Eva smiled and flicked her hair over her shoulder, buoyed by the compliment.

"Thanks, sweetie."

His loss or not, it still stung, but not for the reasons Eva would have thought. Jeff not showing up had a lot less to do with her ego and a whole lot more to do with the deep ache of loss she was feeling inside.

She should have followed her instincts and stuck with the fake date. Relationships were safer that way. She pulled her cell phone out and tapped out a quick text to Troy. Maybe he hadn't ordered yet.

She looked beautiful. Jeff stood and watched Eva for a moment before going into the restaurant. He'd wrestled with showing up at all. It would be torture to sit and watch her, this girl he couldn't help but fall for, with some other man's arm around her. He knew it would test every reserve of patience and self-control he had to sit so close to her and not close the distance between them, reach over and stroke the soft skin of her hand, or even better, kiss her.

But ultimately, he knew what his choice would be and when he got out of the shower, he'd reached for a clean pair of jeans, and a crisp new button-up shirt that Morgan had given for him for Christmas. He couldn't stay away.

However, all his indecision had him running late and even when he'd arrived at the restaurant and had seen only Eva sitting at the table, something held him back from going in right away. Where was her boyfriend? Maybe she'd changed her mind about him because she, too, had felt what he had out in the woods? Maybe Troy was simply in the restroom or running late. Maybe…it didn't matter.

Regardless, it was his chance. She was alone and he was sick of the games. He wasn't going to let one more opportunity go by before telling Eva how he felt. Even if he couldn't quite figure it out himself. He took a deep breath, straightened his shirt and…

"Well, don't you look handsome," a silky voice purred behind him.

He knew exactly who was standing behind him before he turned around. "Marianne. What are you doing here?"

The raven-haired beauty threw herself into his arms, leaving Jeff no choice but to accept her embrace. He instinctively took two steps to the side to keep her out of view in case Eva looked up.

He peeled her off his front and stepped back, needing space between them.

"Sugar, when you didn't answer my emails and weren't returning my calls, you didn't leave me much choice, did you?" she said, her voice washing over him exactly in the way it was intended. Marianne was a master of getting what she wanted.

"When did you get here?" Jeff glanced backwards. Eva was talking to the waiter, a beautiful smile on her face. She didn't seem too bothered that he was late, but that would change if he took too much time with Marianne. Eva didn't seem like the type of woman who would respond well to being stood up.

"Does it matter when I got here, sugar? The fact is, I'm here now." She ran a finger down his chest, pausing on each button. "You're sure looking good." She raised her eyes to meet his, but he quickly looked away. Whatever fleeting relationship, if you could call it that, they'd had during filming, Marianne clearly wanted to pick up where they'd left off.

He grabbed her hand and gently held it in his own, lowering it before letting go. He took another step back, trying to create a bit more distance.

"I have a…a…" He glanced back towards the restaurant.

"A date?" Marianne tried for a playful tone, but Jeff wasn't an idiot. He knew she wouldn't be happy.

"Not a date," he said quickly. He forced himself not to look back at Eva. "But I do have to go. This isn't really a great time to talk. Can I catch up with you tomorrow?"

"Tomorrow?" Marianne stuck her lip out in a first-class pout. "I drove all this way to see you and this is the reception I get?"

He still hadn't made a decision about the job. Not really. And he knew enough about women like Marianne to know that the decision would be made for him if he wasn't careful. There really wasn't a choice. "Okay," Jeff said. "But I'm really in the mood for beer and a burger from the pub. I know that's not really your style, but—"

"I love burgers," she purred. Jeff knew it was a lie, but he let it go.

"Great." He pasted a smile on his face. "You go on ahead and get us a table. There's just a quick thing I need to take care of, and I'll meet you there in five minutes."

"Five minutes?" She lowered her eyelashes and fluttered them in a way that was likely supposed to be alluring, but Jeff found incredibly irritating. Next to Eva, he couldn't be sure what he ever saw in Marianne. Both city girls, Marianne's beauty couldn't even come close to what Eva had.

"I promise." He gave her a smile he knew was sexy. Whatever it took to get her out of there before Eva saw the way she was throwing herself at him. It was bad enough he was late, and he'd have to come up with some reason he couldn't stay for dinner, but he did not want to miss his window of opportunity to speak to Eva alone. He was running out of time and he knew it.

"Five minutes, sugar." She closed the space between them, took his face between her hands and kissed him hard before he had a chance to react.

Her perfume filled his senses, threatening to choke him, and her tongue invaded his mouth in a way he was certain would have worked on him two weeks earlier but now simply felt offensive. Without wanting to provoke her, Jeff carefully broke away from the kiss and managed a smile. He looked up from Marianne, his eyes going directly to Eva. She hadn't seen him, but that was probably only because Troy had his arm around her, and was greeting her with a kiss of his own. Only his was on the cheek.

A flare of jealousy flashed through him. If Eva was his, he certainly wouldn't be wasting any opportunity to show her how he felt, especially with a chaste kiss on the cheek.

"Jeff?"

He'd forgotten about Marianne.

"Are you coming?"

He watched for a minute as Troy slid into the seat across from Eva and her face transformed into a smile. Jealousy burned inside, but there was also something else. Resignation. He'd missed his opportunity, and it no longer mattered. The other man made her happy. Eva was smiling and laughing, and no matter how he felt about her, Jeff didn't do that for her. He let out a sigh and turned around.

"Yes," he said to Marianne. "I'm coming."

Chapter Nine

EVA NEEDED COFFEE. Lots of coffee. After a long night with more tossing and turning than actual sleeping, she was going to need mega doses of caffeine to keep herself going and the in-room coffee maker wasn't going to cut it. Especially since she'd finished off those packets hours earlier when she'd finally given up on the idea of getting any sleep at all.

It didn't matter what she did; every thought was haunted by Jeff and how terribly wrong she'd read the situation with him. She probably should have trusted her first instinct, she thought not for the first time. Everything about him was wrong for her. He liked horses; she was pretty sure they were going to attack her. He was big and muscly; she preferred her men svelte and slim. He was rough around the edges; she'd always gone for a highly polished man. He...made her feel something inside she'd never thought possible.

She grabbed her portfolio full of her to-do lists and left her room behind in search of more coffee. After pushing the elevator button for the lobby, she leaned her head against the wall and slowly counted to ten. She had to get him out of her head. It didn't matter what he made her feel; he didn't feel the same way. That was made clear the night before when he couldn't even be bothered to show up for dinner.

The elevator was mercifully empty, allowing Eva a few more moments of peace. Facing anyone without an appropriate amount of caffeine was a recipe for disaster, especially when her emotions were so jagged.

"I'm glad I found you," Carmen said to her the moment she stepped into the lobby. And then to herself, "I feel like I say that all the time." She shook her head and Eva laughed.

"I know the feeling," Eva said. "What's up?"

Carmen grabbed Eva by the crook of the arm and led her through the room. "I think something's wrong with Andi."

Eva's internal alarm went off but she let the other woman continue.

"She's not eating and she's actually complaining about the food, sending things back, even. She never does that and Bruno is not pleased."

Eva groaned. She'd forgotten all about the issue over the wedding menu. She flipped her clipboard open and put an asterisk next to that item on her list. She'd go talk to Bruno right away.

"Bruno did say something about that," Eva said. "I'll talk to her and get it sorted out."

"It's not just the food, Eva. She's crying all the time and freaking out over the smallest things. I've never seen her like this. Not even when she's here planning the biggest events."

Eva stopped and gave Carmen her biggest, most reassuring smile. "You've also never seen Andi preparing for her own wedding," she said. "All while dealing with her family, which can be challenging, to say the least." Carmen nodded in agreement. "And without Colin," Eva added. "Has he arrived yet?"

Carmen smiled and nodded. "Yes. Thank goodness. He got here last night and I thought Andi might explode with emotion."

"Let me guess," Eva said. "She cried?"

Carmen raised her eyebrow. "You probably think I'm crazy," she said. "But I just have a feeling that something isn't right, and I think of you girls as more than just guests or business partners. You're friends. And I hate to see my friends unhappy."

"I get it," Eva said. And she did. Was Andi really unhappy? Sure, she'd seemed to be stressed out and maybe a bit more emotional than Eva had ever seen her. But unhappy? The thought hit her hard. She'd been so caught up in her own drama with Jeff that she hadn't been paying proper attention to her friend. What kind of best friend was she?

"I'll go see her right now," Eva promised. "And I know Andi would appreciate your concern. Honestly, we both do. You are a good friend, Carmen."

For a moment, Eva thought Carmen herself might break into tears, so she pulled her into an impromptu hug. When she released her, Eva took a long look at her friend, and said, "How about you, Carmen? When was the last time you had a break?"

Carmen waved away Eva's concern. "I don't need a break," she said. "All I have to do to recharge is look at the windows. Besides, this place would fall apart without me."

True enough, Eva thought as she left Carmen at the front desk. And Andi was going to fall apart if Eva didn't figure out what was going on with her.

Grateful for the distraction of the horses, Jeff pulled himself out of bed early and headed for the stables. It's not like he'd slept much anyway. After Marianne had kept him out all night, trying every trick she could think of to get him in bed, he'd managed to fake a headache and get away from her.

It was a good thing he'd stuck to only a few beers or he'd be feeling a whole lot worse than he already was.

And he was feeling like crap. But not because of what little alcohol he may have drunk. No matter what he might try to tell himself, he knew exactly what had his stomach churning and his chest aching. Eva.

For a split second the night before, he'd let himself get his hopes up and think that she wasn't with Troy, that maybe whatever they'd shared together was real. It sure as hell felt real to him. But Marianne had screwed up whatever chance he might have had to tell Eva how he really felt, and even if he'd had the chance, Eva had a boyfriend. It was a little detail he couldn't ignore. No matter how much he wanted to.

The horses greeted him with a chorus of whinnies and snorts, indicating their pleasure.

"Well, at least you're happy to see me," he said and patted Clover on the nose.

"I'm happy, too." He turned at the tiny voice, but he already knew who it belonged to.

"Ella!" He opened his arms just as the little girl crashed into him. "What are you doing here so early?"

"She insisted," Bo said.

Jeff looked up to see his best friend watching them with a smile on his face. Jeff unwound the little girl's arms, took her hand and walked towards Bo.

"And what brings you here so early?"

"I promised Andi's father I'd take his family for a trail ride." He held up his hands, warding off Jeff's protests. "Don't worry, you don't have to come. I know you're busy with other things. Including..." Bo wiggled his eyebrows.

Jeff handed Ella a carrot and said, "Why don't you give this to Clover? I think she deserves a little treat."

Ella grabbed the carrot and skipped through the stable to find Clover's stall. When she was out of hearing range, Bo tried again. "What have you been busy with, Jeff? I heard you took Eva out into the woods yesterday. What was that all about?"

Jeff shot him a look, grabbed a pitchfork propped up against the wall and started shoveling fresh hay into a nearby stall. "I was doing her a favor," he said. "You weren't around."

"Yeah, I was leading a snowshoe expedition with the kids," Bo said. He grabbed a piece of hay and started chewing on the end.

Jeff didn't like the way Bo was staring at him, like he knew exactly what he was thinking, which was probably pretty true, since Bo knew Jeff better than anyone. But it didn't mean he liked it. Jeff jammed the pitchfork deeper into the pile of hay and doubled his efforts. "Well, it doesn't matter. I was just doing her a favor. She needed something for the wedding and there's no way I was going to let her go out into the woods alone."

"Especially not when you were handy to keep her warm. Right, buddy?"

"Dammit." Jeff tossed the pitchfork against the wall. "It's not like that with us."

"Whoa." Bo held up his hands and took a step back. "I didn't mean to hit a nerve."

Jeff took a breath and looked at his friend. "I'm sorry, Bo. I—"

"All good."

"She has a boyfriend." Jeff spoke the words simply, but there was nothing simple about it. He couldn't get the kiss they'd shared out of his head. It was running on repeat, and every time he thought about it, the urge to re-live it was strong. But it kept coming back to the fact that she'd chosen another man. It didn't matter what he wanted.

"What? I'm sure Andi and Colin didn't say anything about Eva having a boyfriend."

Jeff's heart lifted slightly, but then crashed down when he

remembered reality. "It doesn't matter anyway. I'm not in a situation to start a relationship with anyone, even if I wanted to."

"And you want to?" Bo eyed him with a smirk on his face and Jeff could practically read his mind. Jeff had never wanted a relationship with anyone, ever. He'd always run screaming in the opposite direction, so the very fact he'd used the word probably had Bo's head spinning.

"Like I said." Jeff reached for the pitchfork again and busied himself cleaning out a vacant stall. "It doesn't matter. I took the job." The silence in the stables was suffocating as what he'd just said sunk in.

"You did?" Bo said after a moment. "I think it's great."

"You do?" Jeff turned to look at his friend.

"Well, yeah. I mean, you know I'm going to miss you, but the opportunity is amazing. You'd be crazy to turn it down. Besides that, there's nothing for you here. Not really."

Jeff's thoughts flew to Eva. But even if she had chosen him, she was just visiting. The Lodge wasn't her home either. So why did it feel like he was saying goodbye to her just by taking the job?

"Smile," Bo said. He smacked him on the shoulder. "It's a good thing. When do you leave?"

"Where are you going?"

Both men spun around and looked at Ella. Jeff had forgotten she was there, and had probably heard too much of what he didn't want her to. He crouched down in front of her and took in her little quaking lip as she tried to hide her tears. She was a smart girl, and she'd had too many people leave her in her short life. She knew what was coming.

"Ella," Jeff spoke softly. "You know that you're my special buddy and I'd never leave you, right?"

She nodded. "But you said—"

"I know." He reached up and wiped a stray tear from her

cheek. "But just because I'm going to be moving away from the Lodge doesn't mean I'm going to be leaving you, okay?"

She nodded but more tears fell.

"It's time for me to try something new, is all," Jeff said. His heart cracked a little watching her try so hard to hide her tears, but he knew he couldn't change his mind. "And we'll always be special buddies. No matter what. Promise?"

She nodded again.

"And you know what the really cool thing is?" Jeff asked with a smile. "I'm going to be working with actors and actresses. And celebrity horses."

"Celebrity horses?"

He knew that would pique her interest.

"You bet. They're like super famous horses that have their own dressing rooms and everything."

"No they don't." She swatted him and turned serious. "Do they?"

He nodded solemnly. "And they only drink bottled water and eat organic carrots."

"No they don't," she said again, this time with a giggle.

"Sure they do." Jeff pushed to his feet and took Ella by the hand. "Come on," he said. "Let's get some horses ready for your trail ride before your dad tries to do it himself."

Bo winked at him as they walked past and Jeff managed a smile. He'd miss it. But sometimes you had to move on.

Chapter Ten

EVA KNOCKED TWICE on the door of Andi's suite and waited. She could hear movement inside but nobody answered the door. She tried again and this time added, "Andi! I know you're in there. If you don't want me to reschedule your ceremony in an empty stall in the stables, you better answer the door!"

The stables. Jeff.

She shook her head clear of the thought right as the door opened.

Colin stood in the doorway, looking disheveled, exhausted and very much glad to see her. But maybe it was just that he was happy to see back-up of any kind.

"Eva." He grabbed her into a hug and squeezed as he drew her inside. "Thank goodness you're here. What's wrong with your hand?"

Eva brushed off his concern. "It's nothing. It feels much better. But what's going on here? I had to knock three times."

Colin released her and ran a hand through his already mussed-up hair. "It's Andi. She's losing her mind and won't let me in the bedroom."

Eva stepped towards the room and looked at it warily. "What do you mean by, 'losing it'?"

She knew she'd have to deal with a stressed-out version of Andi, but she wasn't looking forward to dealing with an Andi who was freaking out.

"She told me she was going to try on her dress, so I left her alone and went to the Lodge to get breakfast. When I came back, she was still in the bedroom and wouldn't come out." He pointed to the untouched breakfast still sitting on the counter. "I thought I heard crying, Eva. Crying. Andi doesn't cry."

"Well, when it comes to the wedding dress, all bets are off," Eva said. "Besides, have you noticed that Andi's been a bit, well, emotional lately?"

Colin slumped into a chair and took a muffin out of the paper bag. "To be honest, I've been crazy with work, trying to get the Caribbean division wrapped up before the wedding. And I'm ashamed to admit this, but I've kind of left the planning mostly to her. And with her family in town…oh no." He slapped his palm to his forehead. "I'm such a freaking idiot. I can't believe I didn't see it before. The stress of everything is too much. Her family is enough to send her over the edge on a good day."

Colin heaved himself up from the couch and went to the door. Knocking, he said, "Andi? Come on. Open the door. I'm so sorry I left this all to you. Now, open the door, sweetie."

Eva sighed and pushed him aside. "Let me handle this," she said.

She rapped on the door twice. "Andi. It's me. Open the door. I've had about enough of this. It's time to get to work."

To her surprise, the door slipped open just enough to reveal Andi's tear-streaked face.

Eva took a quick glance back at Colin who held up his hands in reverence at her skills, and she slipped into the room. Eva didn't waste any time. She turned on her heel and assessed the situation. "What is going on? You're getting married in slightly more than twenty-four hours and I don't think you understand exactly what that means."

"I do," Andi sobbed. "That's the whole problem. The wedding is tomorrow and everything is wrong." She threw herself on the bed in a move that was excessively dramatic and as un-Andi like as Eva could possibly imagine. It was then that Eva noticed for the first time that Andi was wearing one of the Lodge robes over her wedding dress. The ivory satin peeked out the bottom, but the robe was securely fastened.

Everything clicked together for Eva. The tears. The dramatics. The dress.

"Stand up," Eva ordered. "Let me see."

Andi shook her head into her pillow. "No. It's terrible."

"Your dress is stunning," Eva said. She gently lifted Andi's arm and tried unsuccessfully to pull her to a sitting position. "You know I wouldn't let you buy a dress that wasn't less than amazing." With such short notice for the wedding, they'd been lucky to find such a perfect wedding dress right off the rack and it fit Andi as if it'd been made for her, with very little alteration. Eva couldn't imagine what could possibly be wrong with the gown. "Let me see."

Eva sank onto the bed and brushed Andi's hair from her tear-soaked face. "I've never seen you like this. What's going on?"

Andi lifted her face. "It doesn't—wait, what's wrong with your hand?"

Eva sighed. The stupid hand was getting annoying. "It's a sprain," she said. "What's wrong with the dress?"

Another look of concern flashed across Andi's face and then she said, "It doesn't fit."

"What do you mean, it doesn't fit?"

"It doesn't fit." Andi pushed herself up and sat cross-legged, causing the dress to stick out awkwardly. "I can't do up the zipper. I swear it fit when we got it, and I know I've been stress eating, but still. I didn't think it was that much. Eva, it's terrible. What am I going to do?"

She made a mental list of all the seamstresses she might be able to get to come up to the Lodge on such short notice, and if needed, although she didn't think it would come to that. "Andi, if I have to ask you again to show me the dress, I'm going to lose it. I can't figure out what we're going to do if you don't let me see, now can I?"

Andi sniffed and pulled herself up off the bed and dropped the robe. "See?" She turned to expose her back to Eva.

The zipper gaped, only a fraction of an inch from zipping up properly. "It doesn't look terrible," she said. "Have you tried a corset?"

"A corset?" Andi glared at her over her shoulder. "Why would I need a corset?"

"Well…" Eva waved at the dress. "It would help. And if you're going to keep stress eating for—"

"Fine," Andi snapped and returned her gaze to the mirror. "Where can we get one?"

"I'll have one sent up by Fed Ex." Eva reached for her portfolio to make a note. "I'll rush it and I'm sure it can be here by tonight."

Andi turned away from the mirror and grabbed Eva's good hand. "Thank you." She blinked hard. "I mean it. I know I'm saying it so much right now. But seriously, thank you."

"You'd do the same for me," Eva said. And they both knew she would, but Eva would actually have to find a man she wanted to be with. Her thoughts flashed unwillingly to Jeff, but even if she did want to be with him, he'd stood her up, making it very clear he didn't want to be with her. "Anyway," she said, changing tracks and focusing on the problems at hand. "How are you doing all this stress eating if you're sending back everything Bruno makes for you?"

Andi blushed and shrugged her shoulders. "Is he mad?"

"You could say that. Now spill. What's going on?"

Andi wiggled her way out of the dress, letting it pool in a puddle of satin on the floor. "All I want is chips and chocolate," she said. "My standard stress foods. And I love Bruno's food, I really do. I don't know what it is…but it's just tasting strange right now." She pulled on the robe and shook out the dress, hanging it up on the hanger. "Can you smooth things over with him?"

"I'm already on it." Eva made another note in her portfolio and snapped it shut. "I'm assuming I can make the final decision on the menu? After all, he needs to start prepping."

"I know, I know. I'm being ridiculous. Go ahead."

"Good. Now go clean up and talk to Colin. He's worried about you." She pulled her friend into a hug.

"I can't wait until it's all over," Andi said. "I just want to be married already."

Eva released her and gave her friend the biggest smile she could. "It's going to be amazing," she said. "I promised you it would be and it will."

If Jeff was going to deal with Marianne, he was going to need sustenance, which is how he found himself in the kitchens of the Lodge, seeking out Bruno. He could have snagged some toast or leftover pizza or something equally unappetizing from the fridges in the employee housing block, but for what he needed to do today, he needed something good.

"Bruno." He slapped the chef on the back in some semblance of a man hug and the other man's face lit up in a genuine smile.

"Jeff. How've you been?" Bruno turned back to his skillet. The smell wafting from whatever he was cooking was making

Jeff's mouth water. "I heard you were living it up Hollywood style. How was that? Meet any movie stars?"

Jeff smiled and eyed up a pile of fresh baked croissants. "A few. Mostly they don't associate with the horse wranglers."

Bruno followed his gaze and glared at him. "Don't even think about it," he said. "You can have a bun." He tossed him a dinner roll from a different basket. "Word around the Lodge is you have a very beautiful woman here."

The image in Jeff's mind landed on Eva and the way her lips tasted on his and the way his body responded to her touch. "She's not here for me," he said after a moment. "Can you hook me up with some breakfast? I'm going to need it." Jeff took a bite of the day-old roll and pretended it was a buttery croissant. "It wouldn't kill you to give me one of those, would it?"

"No. Be happy you get a roll." Bruno waved his towel in the air. "Now, tell me. Carmen said the woman came looking for you. Checked in last night."

Marianne.

"Oh," Jeff said and tried not to frown. "Yes, she did come here for me, but—"

"Nice." Bruno smacked his arm and winked. "No wonder you're looking for a good meal," he said. "I'll hook you up."

Jeff pushed away from the counter he'd been reclining on. "It's not like that, though," he said. "Marianne and I met on the set and she only came up to the Lodge because I wasn't answering her calls and—"

He froze when Eva walked into the kitchen. She was stunning, even with her hand wrapped up in a bandage. But her beautiful smile had been replaced by a frown, and she narrowed her eyes when she saw him. "So, this Marianne. She's the reason you couldn't be bothered to show up last night? I should have known it was another woman," she said, stumbling over the word *woman*.

"Eva, it's not like that and she's not—"

"Jeff was telling me all about his brush with fame," Bruno interjected. "But you look like you have something you need to discuss." He wiped his hands on his apron, and Jeff could have strangled him with it. "Did Andi figure out the details for the wedding meal?"

Eva shot him a look he couldn't quite decipher, and turned her attention to Bruno.

Jeff stepped aside while the two of them discussed plans, choosing instead to rummage through the food prep area, snatching a few pieces of fruit. He didn't interrupt, but he kept one eye on Eva the whole time. She cradled her arm close to her chest and scribbled notes with her good hand. She looked so in control and in her element making the arrangements. Despite the fact she'd barely acknowledged him, he could tell she was absolutely aware of the fact he was standing there. It was in the tilt of her head, her stiff back and the obvious only to him way she refused to look in his direction.

"Thanks, Bruno," Eva said, after what seemed like hours of torture having her so close. "I think we've got it all settled. And again, I'm sorry for Andi. Don't take it personally. She's totally losing her mind with this wedding. I've never seen her like this."

"Well, at least she has you," Bruno said. He kissed Eva on the cheek with affection and handed her a fresh croissant wrapped in a napkin. "Take this, you deserve it."

"What? Oh, come on!" Jeff stepped forward and reached out—to what? Take the croissant from her? Pull her in for a kiss? He didn't know.

Both Bruno and Eva stared at him, and Jeff stepped back, tucking his hands into the back pockets of his jeans to keep him from doing either thing. His hunger was making him crazy. Either that or it was the woman in front of him. "I was just thinking you hadn't chosen Andi's horse yet," Jeff said, trying to cover his tracks. "You should come down to the stables with me."

Eva straightened her shoulders and let out a sharp breath. "I don't think so," she said.

She started walking towards the door and all Jeff could think was that he had to stop her. Even if it was with a bogus excuse.

"That was the deal, Eva. I told you if I was going to consider it, you'd have to pick one out."

His plan worked.

Eva turned around and eyed him, likely trying to figure out what he was up to. "Fine."

Jeff's heart lifted.

"But I don't have time right now. Will it work if I come by after the rehearsal dinner?"

She was testing him; he didn't care.

"That'll work."

Eva put her hand on her hip and cocked her head, evaluating him. "And that will give you enough time to get the horse ready for the ceremony?"

He met her challenge with his eyes and wouldn't look away. "I'll work through the night if I have to."

"Good."

"Good."

"So, I'll see you later?"

"I look forward to it."

Jeff only broke his gaze when she spun around to leave, her blond hair whipping behind her. The scent of cinnamon and apple shampoo left in her wake. Sweet and spicy, just like her.

Long after she disappeared through the door, Jeff watched after her.

Forgetting he wasn't alone, he jumped when Bruno cleared his throat and said, "You got it bad, huh?"

Jeff shook his head and said, "It doesn't matter." He turned around and faced the cook. "Even if I did, she has a boyfriend."

"A boyfriend? Is he here? I haven't seen one." Bruno turned back to his prep table. "Eggs okay?"

Jeff nodded, thankful Bruno was finally going to feed him. "Especially if they go with one of those croissants."

Bruno raised an eyebrow, but didn't object which Jeff took to be a good sign.

"And yes," Jeff continued, "the boyfriend is here. His name is Troy."

Bruno froze, his whisk held up in mid-air. "Tall, blond, yummy as they come, Troy?"

"That's the one. I guess," he added. "I never looked at him like that."

"Oh…I have." Bruno wiggled his eyebrows. "Yummy."

"Well, whatever. He's with Eva." It was hard to follow along with Bruno's train of thought, particularly when the smell emanating from his pan was so delicious. And Jeff really had heard enough about how yummy Eva's boyfriend was.

Bruno gave the eggs one more whip and dumped them in a sizzling skillet. "That's where you're wrong, my friend."

Jeff perked his head up. "What do you mean?"

"He's gay."

"Gay?"

"Trust me, I know," Bruno said. He tossed in a handful of cheese and chives and gave the pan a deft shake, causing the eggs to flip over. "I kind of have radar for these types of things, ya know?"

"Uh huh." Jeff's mind raced. Troy couldn't be gay; he was Eva's boyfriend. And if he was, did she know? Would she be humiliated to find out her boyfriend was gay? His temple pulsed at the thought. "You're sure?"

"Oh yeah. I'm sure." Bruno slid the eggs onto a plate, tucked a sprig of parsley and a precisely cut strawberry for garnish on the side and handed it over to Jeff who'd suddenly lost his appetite. "Eat."

He shook his head. "I'm still trying to figure this out. Why would Eva be with a gay man?"

"If I tell you what I think, you better eat. I don't make my special omelettes for just anyone, you know."

Jeff picked up the fork and cut off a corner. "Deal." It did smell fabulous.

"It's fake," Bruno said simply.

"Fake?"

"Exactly. They're not really dating."

"That doesn't make sense. Who would she be…what would she be…" Jeff stared at Bruno, but didn't really see him.

"Eat," his friend commanded and Jeff put a bite in his mouth.

The eggs tasted amazing, and Jeff's appetite came roaring back. He took another bite and then another.

"Better," Bruno said. "Now as for your girl, I can't tell you why she's with him. Women are confusing. So that's your detail to discover. Now fuel up and get out of here. I have a lot of work to do." He tossed a croissant onto Jeff's plate and went back to work.

"Thanks, buddy."

Bruno waved his hand in the air, but didn't turn around.

Jeff wolfed down the last of his eggs and took the croissant. Bruno had given him a lot to think about because if Eva wasn't really with Troy, that meant there was nothing keeping them apart.

Except Eva herself.

It had been a busy day and she'd taken care of the dinner arrangements, made sure the decorations were complete, ordered and received the corset for Andi—which she still wasn't pleased about—and with Troy's help, made sure the centerpieces were complete.

Everything was ready. Except for the horse.

Keeping busy all day meant Eva didn't need to think about Jeff, the kiss they'd shared and pretty much all the rest of the drama and questions that seemed to come up whenever she thought about him.

It was easier to keep busy.

Which is exactly what she intended to do. She put the final touches on her makeup as best she could with the use of only one arm. Her sore wrist was feeling better, and with any luck she could take the bandage off for the ceremony in the morning. Eva examined herself in the mirror. She'd never put so much energy into her appearance before and it's not like Jeff would care, even if he did notice.

But he wouldn't be impressed anyway, she thought as she smoothed her good hand over her black pants and assessed her teal sweater. He'd only be impressed if she was in jeans and a flannel shirt, with big clunky winter boots. And that wasn't going to happen. Not for Andi's rehearsal dinner, anyway.

Eva smiled inwardly at the thought of her dressing like a ranch hand. It probably wouldn't be too bad, if Jeff was there to help her get undressed.

"No," she spoke to her reflection. "Not now. Not him. Not happening."

Before she could let her imagination get carried away again, Eva snatched up her purse, leaving her clipboard behind for once, and headed down to Oliver's, the Lodge's premier restaurant, where they'd rented out the entire back room for Andi's festivities.

Almost everyone was there by the time Eva pushed her way into the room. Andi's family took up more space than she would have thought. What with the twins running around and her father and mother doing their best to pretend the other didn't exist, the room seemed a lot smaller than it was.

"I'm so glad you're here," Andi said, grabbing Eva by the arm.

"Hey. Sorry I'm late. You look great. Are you feeling better, then?"

When Andi smiled, her whole face lit up. She positively glowed. "So much! I don't know if I just needed some rest, or Colin by my side, or what it was. But I feel fine now. Thank you for putting up with my craziness."

"Hey, I've had years of practice." She winked at her, and then scanned the room again. "Have you seen Troy?"

"Troy?"

"Colin's friend…my date. Tall, blond, crazy good looking. The one you wanted me to date. Have you seen him?"

"Oh him," Andi said, genuinely surprised. "I'd totally forgotten about him."

"Clearly." Eva strained her neck to look over her friend's shoulder and see if she could spot him. "He was supposed to meet me here."

Andi smiled and looked at her strangely. "Really? So you guys hit it off then?" she asked, after a moment. "You know, I always kind of thought he was gay."

Eva snapped to attention but avoided her friend's gaze. "Why would you want to set me up with him if he was?"

Andi shrugged, bored with the topic. "Sometimes I'm wrong about these things," was all she gave for an answer. "Anyway, I'm glad you found each other then."

Right, Eva thought. They'd found each other all right and it had seemed like such a good idea at the time, but the longer the fake date scenario played out, the harder it would be to come clean to Jeff and see what there was between them. If there was anything at all.

That was the ultimate question plaguing Eva. The one she

couldn't let go of. Keeping up the illusion with Troy was easy because he was safe. And Jeff was anything but safe. And everything that she wanted.

"Earth to Eva." Andi waved a hand in front of her and she quickly put a smile on her face, focusing on the situation.

"Sorry," she said. "I was just thinking about some last-minute details."

"You're a terrible liar," Andi said. She giggled and Eva joined in because Andi was right.

Fortunately, Eva was saved from having to explain anything because at that moment Andi's dad clinked on his glass and the entire room hushed to listen to his toast.

"I just want to take a moment to raise a glass to my beautiful daughter and the man lucky enough to marry her."

A murmur of agreement and laughter traveled through the crowd.

"You are perfect together and it does my heart good to see how in love you both are." He pulled a handkerchief out of his pocket and cleared his throat loudly. "May you have a long, healthy life, filled with happiness and many babies running…"

Eva didn't hear the rest of the toast, because she'd fixated on one word. She turned to Andi, who clearly had come to the same conclusion. "Babies?" They mouthed the word to each other and Eva's eyes dropped to her best friend's stomach.

Chapter Eleven

JEFF COULDN'T FOCUS on anything all day. His brain flitted from one thing to the next without landing on one task for more than five minutes. It made getting any real work done next to impossible and after hours of wasted day, he finally gave up, saddled up Clover and took her for a ride.

The sky was gray, and the clouds hung heavy and low on the mountains. A storm was coming, which wasn't surprising for January, particularly since they hadn't had a good dump of snow for weeks.

Not wanting to push his luck with the weather, Jeff rode only far enough to clear his head before turning back. It didn't take as long as he thought. Riding always worked to make him feel better, even if every thought he had was still of Eva.

Only a few more hours and he was going to get to the bottom of whatever it was with her, or more likely, whatever it was that was keeping them apart.

"Women. Hey, Clover?" He patted the horse's neck and she let out a snort in response. "Maybe if I could get her out for a ride on you she'd see how we can make this work. That is, if she liked horses."

Clover jerked her neck, as if in response to that tidbit of news.

"I know, I know." He patted her neck. "But I think we can change that. Don't you?"

He barely had to lead the horse back to the stables. She knew exactly where she was going and it was an easy ride that allowed Jeff to think about everything he was going to give up by leaving.

He allowed himself to look around, taking in everything and committing it to memory.

"I'm going to miss you, girl," he said to Clover. Anyone listening may have thought he'd completely lost his mind, but he didn't care. Talking to Clover had always been therapeutic. "But you won't be able to get rid of me that easily. I'll be back. And you never know, I might even bring someone famous back with me."

Jeff took the lack of response from his favorite horse as consent for him to leave. As Clover walked through the fence into the yard, Jeff knew he'd made the right decision. At least as far as the job was concerned. Eva was a different story altogether. But he'd figure that out, too. First, he needed to find Marianne, and make things official.

As it turned out, Marianne wasn't too hard to find. After Jeff got Clover back into the stables and gave her some fresh feed, he made his way up to the Lodge, where he found her waiting in the main room. She lounged by the fireplace, looking every bit the Hollywood maven in her fancy clothes and full makeup. Instead of getting up, she raised a finger when she spotted him.

"Hey," he said. "Shouldn't you be getting ready to head back?"

She patted the cushion next to her and gave him a slow smile. "That depends," she said, her voice a low purr. "Are you going to give me a reason to stay?"

Opting to stand, Jeff leaned against the arm of the sofa. "I told you I'd take the job," he said. "And I'm ready to sign the contract. Do you have it ready?"

"Sugar, I'm always ready." She lowered her eyelids and batted them in a way he had no doubt worked for most men. Heck, it'd worked for him once.

"The papers?"

"Right here, sugar." She slid a packet from her attaché case and held them out with two red manicured fingers.

Jeff snatched them from her and flicked through them, giving them a cursory look. He already knew what they said. He'd seen a copy earlier.

"Pen?"

Marianne reached into her case again and withdrew a ballpoint pen. "My, my," she said. "You're all business today." She held the pen out.

"I'm very busy." Jeff reached out to grab it, but she pulled it back. He caught himself before he fell onto her.

"Too busy for me?" she purred.

He knew he had two options. He could make it hard, or he could try to minimize the damage.

"You know I'm never too busy for you, Marianne." Jeff gave her the smile he knew would melt her, and sure enough, a smile of her own crossed her face and she handed him the pen.

Before she could snatch it back, Jeff signed next to his name and added the date. "I'm in," he said.

Surprising even himself, a sense of calm washed over him. He handed the papers back to her, and he knew with a certainty he hadn't had before he'd made the right choice. He'd miss the Lodge without a doubt, but it was time to move on.

"I'm so glad you signed, sugar." Marianne pulled herself up from the couch with a fluidity that Jeff wasn't sure was humanly possible and closed the gap between them. "We can pick up right where we left off." She ran a red fingernail down the side of his face, and he fought the urge to shudder.

They'd left off in a rather uncomfortable situation involving each of them entwined in sheets, and only Marianne happy to be there. Sure, it'd been a good idea at the time— wasn't it always? But waking up next to Marianne felt wrong and he tried to let her down easy at the time. Or at least, he thought he had. Jeff took her hand gently in his own and lowered it. "I don't think so."

Her face twisted in what could only be considered a grimace. "What do you mean?"

"Things have changed," he said. "Besides, I don't think it's a good idea to get involved with people I work with."

"Nonsense." Marianne slid herself even closer, pressing up against his chest until his senses were assaulted by the strength of her perfume. "Everyone in the industry is involved. It really isn't an issue."

He took a step back and gulped a breath of fresher air. "It is for me. I'm sorry."

Marianne straightened and put one hand on her hip, assessing him. "I see what's going on," she said.

"You do?" A cross between panic and relief flooded through him. Maybe this would be over without any dramatics.

"You're married, aren't you?"

"Married?" Jeff reeled. "No. I'm not married."

"But there is someone else?"

Was there? Of course there was, at least in his mind. "Yes." He nodded. "At least I'd like there to be."

Marianne nodded slowly, and her eyes raked over him. "I see," she said, although Jeff was pretty sure she didn't. "Well, if that's the way it is, then that's the way it is." She picked up her purse and slung it over her shoulder. "I guess I'll see you on set, then."

"Thank you," he said. "For understanding, I mean. I really am looking forward to working together, and—"

She held up a finger to silence him. "It doesn't really matter, does it?" She walked away, her high heels clicking on the slate floor, before Jeff could even figure out what she'd meant.

As soon as dessert was over and the speeches concluded, Eva said her goodbyes, and under the excuse of tying up the details for the ceremony, she escaped the rehearsal dinner. But not before whispering in Andi's ear that they would talk in the morning about what they both suspected. Surprisingly, Andi didn't seem worried or stressed by the thought that she might be pregnant. In fact, the realization seemed to have the opposite effect on her. She'd been smiling and more relaxed than she had been all week.

But then again, why should she be stressed? Andi was marrying the man of her dreams in less than twenty-four hours. A baby would only be an added blessing to them. Not a reason for worry.

"I'll be by first thing tomorrow to help you get ready," Eva said. "Have a great evening. It's your last one as Andi Williams."

"Don't I know it?" Her smile was huge and contagious. "Where are you headed to now? I thought everything was ready for tomorrow?"

"It is," Eva said quickly. She didn't need the bride concerned about anything. "There's just one little detail I need to take care of with Jeff."

"Is that right? And what might that be?"

Eva swatted her friend on the shoulder. "Stop it. I need to choose your horse, is all. Besides, you know that Troy is my date tomorrow." The lie felt toxic on her tongue and by the look on Andi's face, she knew it too.

"About that," Andi said. "Turns out that Troy is gay. Colin got a good laugh out of it when I told him you were dating him." She emphasized the word *dating*. "So maybe your trip to see the horses tonight is about a little more than just my ride tomorrow?"

Eva looked away, not ready to tell Andi anything. Not when she didn't even understand things herself. "I'll see you in the morning," she said, and gave Andi one last hug.

She wasn't sure what to expect when she arrived at the stables, and she was certainly no more dressed for it than she was the first time she'd ventured down, but there was a nervous anticipation in her belly. And even though Eva wasn't sure what was going on between her and Jeff, she couldn't stop thinking about the kiss, and the way it had twisted her insides in a very good, incredibly exciting way.

But she'd have to tell Jeff the truth about Troy, because the other thing Eva couldn't stop thinking about was the look on Jeff's face when he'd seen her with Troy's arm around her shoulders. And he hadn't shown up for dinner either, so maybe she was wrong about everything. Maybe he really did only want to talk to her about the horse.

"Hello," Eva called out as she picked her way across the yard. The only light was coming from the barn, so despite her better judgment about being so close to a building full of horses, she headed towards them. "Jeff?" she called as she got to the door. The large sliding door was open a crack, so she poked her head in and almost jumped out again.

There were at least six horse heads hanging out of the stalls and they all turned towards her when she stepped inside. But Jeff was there as well. And his presence was the only thing keeping her from turning and running before the horses could hurt her. She knew she was being irrational, but she couldn't seem to stop herself.

"Hey," Jeff said. His face split into a genuine smile when he saw her and something inside Eva calmed. At least he was happy to see her. He stepped forward and held his hand out to her.

She took a tentative step inside and took his hand. She had to resist the urge to close her eyes and savor the sensation of his warmth. There was something protective and safe about his presence and being near him allowed her to relax.

"There's nothing to be worried about," Jeff said, reading her body language. "I know you said you didn't like horses, but I can't believe how tense you are. I promise, they won't hurt you. Not unless you're twelve and at summer camp."

She couldn't help but laugh at how silly she was being. "Point made."

"It really is okay," Jeff said. His voice was soothing but the way he looked at her was anything but calm.

"I wanted to tell—"

"Let me show—"

They spoke at the same time. "You first," Eva said. She'd wanted to clear the air right away, but maybe the time wasn't right. She'd wait. They should probably take care of things with the horses first.

Jeff looked at her strangely, but continued. "Okay," he said. "Come with me. I want to show you how gentle these guys are." He led her down the center of the barn, and stopped in front of a stall with a completely white horse. "This is Snowball."

"Snowball?"

"I know. It's not the most creative name, but when she was born it fit. She was like a little ball of snow."

Eva looked up at him in amazement. "You were here when she was born?"

He nodded. "She's only a few years old, and she was born right here at the Lodge. So I was lucky enough to be around for the big day. She's beautiful, isn't she?"

Eva returned her gaze to the horse, and had to admit, she was a pretty good-looking animal. She nodded. "Is she the one you think would be good for the wedding?"

Jeff patted the horse's nose. "Don't you?"

She took a long look at the horse and nodded. "Actually, I think she'd be beautiful. That is, if you're going to let Andi have a horse in the wedding."

Jeff grinned. "I was always going to let Andi have the horse," he said. "But I needed a reason to get you down here."

"What?" She tried to look mad, but she was pretty sure he'd be able to see through her act.

"I wanted you to see for yourself how amazing the horses could be."

She returned his smile and on her own, reached out to stroke Snowball. They stood in silence for a few moments, and Eva was just about to spill the truth about Troy when Jeff surprised her by asking, "Do you want to ride her?"

"Do I what?" Eva shook her head and instinctively backed off.

"It's totally safe," he said. "She's really gentle."

"I'm sure she is." Eva forced herself to take a deep breath. "But I'm not really dressed for it."

Jeff looked down and took in her outfit. His eyes slowly worked their way up and held hers again. "You look perfect to me," he said softly.

Neither of them looked away and Eva couldn't think of any other objections.

"You said yourself she was beautiful," Jeff reasoned. "And you can see how gentle she is. Here." He took her hand and gently placed it on the horse's head. Her first instinct was to withdraw and run, but Snowball was soft, almost like velvet, and she felt nice under Eva's hand.

After a moment, Eva tentatively moved her fingers, surprising herself with how much she enjoyed the feel of the animal. She barely noticed when Jeff took his hand away, and she was touching Snowball on her own.

"She's so soft," Eva whispered, as if afraid to break the spell.

"She is, isn't she? And she absolutely loves to be scratched behind the ears. Watch." Snowball lowered her head, and Jeff obliged by rubbing her. The horse whinnied her approval and Eva slid her hand up to reach the horse's ears.

"She likes it," Eva whispered.

"See? So how about that ride? You know, to make sure she'll be safe for Andi's big day?"

Eva surprised herself by not immediately saying no. Instead, she looked at Jeff, and knew she could completely trust him. He wouldn't let her fall off and break her arm. She knew that without a doubt.

"Okay."

"Okay?"

Eva nodded. "Okay."

Jeff's face lit up as if she'd just told him he'd won the lottery, and he sprang into action. "Let me go grab the saddles. It will just take a moment to get her ready."

Eva watched as he moved about, readying the horses. He saddled up Snowball and a dappled horse he called Clover for himself. She thought she'd be terrified to mount the horse, but when Jeff led them all outside into the cool winter night, and boosted her up into the saddle, she felt strangely at peace. Something about Jeff and the quiet night soothed her, which almost made her laugh since only days earlier everything he'd said irritated her. Or had it? Hadn't she loved the way he challenged her? Wasn't that part of the attraction she couldn't deny?

She didn't have time to analyze it any further because Snowball whinnied beneath her and when Jeff and his horse started moving, Snowball followed behind. It took every bit of concentration for Eva to focus on staying on the horse. She squeezed her thighs tightly, and closed her eyes.

"She knows where she's going," Jeff said. "But you should open your eyes. You wouldn't want to miss this," Jeff said, his voice light. "Look around."

She did. And immediately sucked her breath in. The snow that had threatened earlier had started falling while they were inside. The moon lit up the snow-covered ground and with the gentle flakes falling from the sky, the whole effect was magical.

"It's like we're in a snow globe," Eva said. She tilted her face up to the sky and let the cold flakes melt on her hot skin. The horse moved slowly beneath her and she let her body meld into the movement. "This is amazing."

Jeff pulled Clover up so the horses were walking side by side. "Do you see now why I wanted you to try it?"

Eva lowered her head and looked him in the eyes. "Thank you for convincing me. It's not nearly as bad as when I was a kid."

They laughed together, but then a thought crossed Eva's mind. "But why did it mean so much to you that I get on the horse?" She hoped she knew the answer, but she wanted to hear it from him.

Jeff looked down and ran a gloved hand through his hair. "I wanted you to know how amazing it could be and I needed you to trust me because I…" He trailed off.

"You?"

He opened his mouth and Eva held her breath. It's a good thing the horse knew where she was going, because Eva couldn't focus on anything but the man on horseback next to her.

He shook his head and muttered something to himself. "It doesn't matter."

"What?"

"You have a boyfriend and I shouldn't—"

"I don't."

He didn't seem to hear her. "I never would have kiss—"

Relying on instincts, Eva jerked back on the reins, bringing Snowball to an abrupt stop and eliciting a whinny of protest from her. "I don't have a boyfriend," Eva said, raising her voice to be heard. "Troy agreed to be my fake date to keep Andi from trying to set me up all the time. I'd just broken it off with…it doesn't matter. What matters is…Jeff? Look at me, please."

He'd already brought his horse to a stop beside hers, but he still hadn't looked up.

"Jeff." Eva tried again. "What matters is, that kiss, it was…well…"

When she didn't finish, Jeff finally looked up, and with a smirk on his face he asked, "It was what?"

"You knew." Eva narrowed her eyes and tipped her head, assessing his demeanor. "You knew Troy wasn't my boyfriend."

He nodded. "I knew," he agreed. "Sorry, I wanted to see if you'd tell me and…well, I couldn't keep a straight face."

"I see that." She tried to look mad, but he looked so handsome sitting there in the saddle with snow falling around him, all she really wanted to do was kiss him again.

"But I didn't always know," he said, turning serious. Jeff maneuvered his horse so they were as close as they could be without actually touching. "When I saw you with him the other day, after we kissed. I hated it. It tore me up. You've been driving me crazy, Eva. I've never met a woman like you and… oh, forget it."

In one swift move, he reached out and wrapped his arm around her, pulling him towards her. His lips, cool from the night air, were on hers and instantly she melted into him. He held her firm, and even with the jostling of the horses, she knew he wouldn't let her go. She focused completely on the taste of him, and the earthy smell of him she couldn't get enough of, as they explored each other's mouths. The kiss was passionate, but there was also a sweetness in it. Like he was telling her exactly how he felt, and she responded in kind.

It was over too soon. He pulled away, trailing his fingers across her cheek before leaning back. She righted herself in the saddle and took a moment to catch her breath.

"We should probably get the horses back," he said.

Eva tried to hide her disappointment, but he must have read it on her face.

"Besides," Jeff added. "The sooner we get back, the sooner I can kiss you properly."

With a smile on her face, Eva didn't even notice the biting cold as the wind picked up on their way back. The heat from Jeff's kiss lingering on her lips was all she needed to keep warm.

Chapter Twelve

IT HAD BEEN difficult to fall asleep with Jeff's kiss lingering on her lips, and the warm, tingling feeling that traveled from her core to every part of her. Was that love? Or just the excitement from riding a horse and finally connecting with the man she couldn't get off her mind? Whatever it was, Eva had never felt it before. Unless you counted that boy in the six grade who'd tugged on her braid and kissed her on the cheek before running off, and she didn't.

Somehow, Eva managed to get a few hours' sleep before the chaos of the wedding day ensued. She took her time in the shower, knowing it would likely be the only peace and quiet she got all day, but as soon as she turned the water off, she was in full party planner mode. Eva rushed through her morning rituals and before she got dressed, bent her bad wrist up and down a few times, deciding she shouldn't have to wrap it up. It was feeling a lot better, and she was going to be so busy, she wouldn't even have time to think about the pain if there was any. Eva grabbed her trusty portfolio and the garment bag containing her maid of honor dress, and then took off for

Andi's condo. But first she had one little stop to make at the village corner store.

Twenty minutes later, she was standing in the kitchen of Andi's condo with two steaming cups of coffee, fresh bagels, and a pregnancy test.

"The box says it will only take three minutes," Eva said, pushing it towards her friend.

"I don't think I want to know."

"Now? Or ever?"

Andi put her hand on her hip. "Not ever, obviously. But with everything else going on today, it might just be too much."

Eva took a sip of coffee and gave Andi a second to think about it. "Okay," she said after a minute. "You and Colin both want kids, right?"

Andi nodded.

"This is a good thing."

"We don't even know what the test will say," Andi argued.

"I think we both know exactly what the test will say." She pushed the box towards her again. "Wouldn't it be good to know for sure?"

Andi stared at her for a minute. "You're right." She snatched up the box and headed to the bathroom.

"Thank goodness," Eva mumbled under her breath.

The weather was perfect for an outdoor ceremony. It was one of those January days where there was a chill in the air, but it wasn't unbearably cold. And with the sky so blue and the sun sparkling off the snow and the frozen pond, the setting was so beautiful that nobody noticed if they were a little chilly.

Eva stood in her dress covered by a floor-length red wool coat. Her black gloves contrasted with it sharply as she held a bouquet of roses, sprigs of pine, and of course, holly. She smiled at Troy, who was standing up for Colin, and he gave her a wink. When the music changed, they both turned to watch as Andi rode down the path on Snowball. Jeff had obviously brushed her and prepared her for the ceremony with some extra attention, because the horse looked amazing. But not as stunning as Andi. When she reached the end of the aisle, Jeff was there to take her hand and help her from the horse. Eva couldn't help but stare at him. Totally unaffected by the cool air, he was dressed in only a black suit with a red shirt. It was a far cry from the faded jeans and old t-shirts Eva was used to seeing him in and that warm tingly feeling rushed back through her limbs.

He didn't look up before guiding the horse away, and Eva stared after him for just a moment before turning her attention back to her best friend, who was walking up the aisle with her father, looking more beautiful than Eva had ever seen her. She glanced at Colin, and saw his eyes shining full of love as he watched his bride walk towards him. It was one of the single most amazing moments Eva had been part of. To witness love so pure, and so consuming that it was the only thing that mattered, was exhilarating.

Her own eyes filled up with tears and she blinked hard to keep them at bay. The justice of the peace called the service to order, and mercifully, Eva could focus on the words he spoke, allowing herself to be distracted long enough not to cry at the beauty of the moment. She glanced around briefly, trying to locate Jeff, and finally spotted him standing to the side of the small crowd. He was focused on the ceremony and Eva couldn't help but wonder what was going through his head. Was he thinking of the power of love as well? Was he perhaps wondering if maybe that's what they shared together?

The idea was ridiculous, of course. After all, they hadn't even had a proper date. They barely even knew each other. But Eva couldn't help herself from letting her mind wander. Jeff was different. Things with him were different. She closed her eyes and listened to the justice of the peace speak about Andi and Colin and their love for each other, and the mental image that formed was of her and Jeff. Together. She didn't care if she was being ridiculous and jumping into things; it was right. And she knew it. She felt it.

Eva snapped her eyes open, looking back to where Jeff stood, eager to make eye contact with him.

Instead of standing by himself, a tall dark-haired woman was draped on his arm. She was whispering in his ear and running a red fingernail down his cheek. Nausea churned in her stomach at the sight, but she couldn't turn away. She watched as Jeff turned to the woman and whispered something in her ear that made the woman throw back her head in a silent laugh. And then, the woman reached forward and kissed him.

Eva let out a sharp gasp, and then immediately covered her mouth, turning her attention back to the vows that were about to take place. She managed a small smile and mumbled an apology, and the ceremony continued. But Eva could no longer focus. The tears she'd been holding in slipped out and down her cheek. Only she couldn't be sure anymore if the tears were for Andi and Colin, or her and the physical ache in her core. How was it possible to feel such a high followed by such a crashing low? Eva swallowed hard; she built her courage, needing to know if she'd seen what she thought she had. She glanced again to where Jeff stood, but he was gone. Along with the beautiful mystery woman.

Eva forced herself to pay attention to what was happening in front of her, and willed herself to focus. Soon, the justice of the peace pronounced the couple husband and wife, and when they kissed, the small crowd erupted in a cheer. When they pulled apart, Eva heard Andi whisper to Colin, and put his hand on her stomach, just as she said she would. And when

Colin whooped in joy, Eva, caught up in their moment, did too. Watching her best friend's world come together and the creation of a new family full of love, for just a second, her own heartbreak no longer mattered.

Andi and Colin danced their way down the aisle to the cheers and applause of their friends and family, and for a moment, Eva forgot what she was supposed to do. It wasn't until Troy took her arm and looped it through his that her feet started moving automatically.

"Smile," he whispered to her. "This is a happy day."

"I know, but—"

"I saw," he said simply. "I saw."

Eva looked up and saw the pity and friendship in Troy's eyes and almost started to cry again. She forced a smile and squeezed his arm closer. She should have gone with her first instinct after all, and stuck with her fake date.

Chapter Thirteen

JEFF NODDED and smiled at the wedding guests, most of whom he'd never met, and tried his best to push his way through the crowd without being rude. He needed to find Eva. She'd looked incredible standing next to Andi with her red coat and her blond hair swept back off her face. From the moment he saw her, all he wanted to do was twist his fingers through that amazing hair, kissing her so thoroughly that it became unpinned and fell down her back in a wild tangle.

Watching her, he'd been fixated, unable to stop thinking about holding her, kissing her...but then Marianne had come out of nowhere and destroyed his private reverie. He'd done his best to get rid of her without making a scene. But Lord knows that wasn't easy when you were dealing with a woman like Marianne. She was supposed to have gone home. She was the last person he'd expected to see, or wanted to, and worse, she wouldn't take no for an answer. As it turned out, he'd forgotten to initial a page on the employment contract. At least that's what her cover story was. Just to be sure, when he'd finally managed to drag her away from the ceremony, Jeff made it clear in no uncertain terms that he wasn't interested. There was someone else.

And was there ever.

Jeff turned around again, scanning the busy reception hall, and there she was.

Forming a small receiving line next to the bride and groom, Eva was standing with the groomsman, Troy. At least now Jeff knew he was a fake date and nothing more. His heart sped up just watching her, and the way she laughed and chatted with guests. She shook hands and smiled, but there was something wrong. She looked like she was acting, holding herself a little too stiffly. Her smile wasn't as bright as he remembered, like she was forcing it.

He needed to speak with her, to see what was wrong and what he could do about putting that smile back where it belonged. But the only way to do that would be to get into the receiving line. Jeff dodged around two young boys who were barreling towards him, and slipped into the line, only about ten people back. Eva looked up from the elderly woman she was greeting, and caught his eye. Jeff smiled but she looked away and focused on the next person in line, her face dropping into a frown.

Jeff recognized who it was a split second too late. Marianne. What the hell was she doing here? He didn't have time to process the question as he watched her lean forward and whisper something into Eva's ear. She stepped back and grinned in Jeff's direction, but he wasn't looking at her. All of his focus was on Eva and the pain that crashed over her face.

"Eva," he called out, remembering a split second too late that he was standing in the middle of a wedding reception. Everyone turned to look in his direction, blocking his view, and impeding his progress through the room. All he could see was her hand rise to her eyes, and Troy wrapping his arm around her bare shoulders while he steered her out of the room. And away from him.

———

"This shouldn't be so hard," Eva said. She blinked hard and dabbed her eyes with a tissue Troy had handed her the moment they'd escaped into the kitchen. "Why do I always pick the losers?"

"I don't think Jeff's a loser." Troy leaned against the door to the walk-in refrigerator and waited while Eva pulled herself together.

She looked up and stared at him in astonishment. "You don't? What would you call a man who starts something with me while he's getting ready to move away with a different woman?"

"I don't think that's the case," he said.

But it was the case. That woman, the same woman who'd cuddled up to Jeff during the ceremony, had told her exactly that. "She said he was moving away to be with her. Why would she make that up?"

"Why would she tell you at all?" Troy countered. "In my experience, if a woman makes a point to mark her territory, there's a reason."

Eva turned and leaned against the prep counter. There were too many possibilities racing through her head, but nothing made sense.

"I just don't know what to think."

"About what?"

Eva spun around as Bruno came in the room.

"And why are you in my kitchen?"

She tried to straighten her dress and at least pretend that she was under control and nothing was wrong.

"You look fine," Troy said. "Doesn't she?"

"You look amazing," Bruno said. "As always." He spoke to Eva, but his eyes were on Troy, and Eva couldn't help but smile at his blatant attraction.

"Would you tell her that not all men are trying to hurt her?" Troy asked the chef.

It took a moment, but Bruno finally shook his head out of whatever daze he'd put himself under and refocused on Eva. "It's true," he said. "Most men are good. What is this about? Or should I ask, who is this about?"

"Jeff," Troy said.

"He's a liar and a cheat and—"

"Jeff? Not our Jeff?" Bruno looked between them both. "The Jeff I know is nothing like that. He's honest and loyal and has the mega hots for you. Does he not?"

"Yes," Eva said. "I mean, no. I thought he did, but—"

"But she's letting someone else change her opinion about everything. Without even giving him a chance to explain," Troy said. "Isn't that about right?"

She shook her head. "No. I mean, I would give him the chance."

"But?"

Eva didn't have an answer for him. She looked down at her feet.

"Eva," Bruno said, his voice gentle. "Jeff is a good man. He wouldn't hurt you. Not on purpose. You know that, don't you?"

She nodded. She did know it. She felt it in his kiss, and in the way he held her. The way he'd guided her and kept her safe on the horse. She'd trusted him then; why not now?

"Good," Bruno announced. "Now get out of here. I have a dinner to prepare for. I do not need an angry bride after me. Especially an angry, pregnant bride."

Eva laughed at the image of Andi chasing the chef down in her wedding gown. "No," she agreed. "You don't need that."

Troy grabbed her hand. "Besides," he said. "I think I hear

the first dance. We don't want to miss that. And we're up next. You owe me a dance, you know?"

She grinned at him. "Okay, but just one. And then your dance card's open." She winked in Bruno's direction and let Troy lead her out to the reception and the dance floor.

***

There was nothing that would keep him away from her again. Not until he'd had a chance to explain and make her understand. So when Jeff saw Troy leading Eva out to the dance floor for the wedding party dance, he made his move. Not willing to risk the wrath of a bride whose plans were interrupted, Jeff was smart enough to wait until the second chorus before he slipped onto the floor and cut in.

"May I?" he asked Troy.

The other man smiled, held out Eva's arm to him and bowed gallantly. "Please, by all means," he said. And then before he walked away, he added quietly, "Be good to her."

Jeff turned and looked into Eva's eyes as he pulled her close, keeping one hand on the small of her back and one hand clasped around hers as he picked up the beat and led them across the dance floor. "You look beautiful," he said. He drank her in, trying to read what was going on behind her beautiful eyes.

She tensed and ducked her head. "Thank you," she said. She didn't sound angry, and Jeff took that as a good sign.

However, she didn't offer anything more, and he didn't immediately push. But after a few beats, he couldn't wait any longer; he needed to know what had happened. He needed to know why she'd closed herself off from him. "I don't know what she said to you," he said. "I don't even know why she's still here, but—"

Eva's head whirled up and her face was tight with anger. "But you do know her?"

They both knew the answer to that question and the only thing that was going to save things between them was honesty. "Yes," he said quietly. "We were together once. But it's over."

Eva glared at him. "That's not the way she tells it." She swallowed hard, and her cheeks pinked with the anger she was holding in. "She told me she was here to pick you up because you were moving away together."

Jeff took an involuntary step back, breaking their rhythm. He caught himself quickly and resumed the dance.

"Is it true?" Eva asked.

"No," he said. "Well, yes." She pulled to break away from him, but Jeff turned it into a spin and pulled her closer. "She made it sound like something it's not," he whispered into her ear. "She hired me to work for a production company that's filming in the city. So I am moving, and I suppose she'll probably be there somewhere since she works for the company, too. But I'm not moving away with her." He pulled away, just enough so she'd be able to look into his eyes when he spoke. "Eva, there is nothing between me and Marianne, despite what she might say or want."

He held his breath, letting her absorb what he'd said. He knew he shouldn't hold back, but he had to see how she'd react, if she would believe him. He needed her to believe him and trust him.

After a moment, her expression melted a bit and he could see that she might be accepting his truth. But then she shook her head. "No," she said and tried to pull away. He wasn't prepared for her response, but there was no way Jeff was going to let her go. He pulled her deftly into a spin and held her back against his chest, one arm wrapped around her stomach. He swayed with the beat of the music, which had changed to a different song. Couples crowded the dance floor around them, but he didn't care.

"Yes," he whispered in her ear. "I don't care about Marianne and what she might have said to you, because I know that whatever this is between us, it's something. From the moment I met you in those impractical and totally sexy boots, I felt it. Even when you were making me crazy, it was because you challenged me, and I loved it. And I don't know what's going to happen from here. But I do know I want to find out, and from the way you kissed me last night, I think you feel exactly the same way. No," he said slowly. "I know you feel the same way."

He knew his breath was hot on her neck and he could feel the shudder go through her. He released her, spinning her around so they were once again chest to chest. This time, one hand held her close, while the other traced the lines of her cheek, and worked their way up to the pin that held her hair in place. "You're beautiful, and hardheaded and absolutely amazing," he said. "Together, there's something between us that's undeniable and—"

"Jeff, I—"

"Tell me it's not true," he challenged. His eyes held hers, and he could see the battle warring in them. "You can't tell me that you don't feel exactly the same way."

"No," she whispered, her voice husky. "I can't tell you that." She paused and looked down. "But I've been hurt before and—"

"I'll never hurt you, Eva." Jeff stopped moving and tipped her head up, forcing her to look at him.

"I know," she said simply. "You make me feel safe and strong all at the same time, even when you irritate me." She smiled a little and moved to close the tiny gap between them.

He met her halfway, their lips crashing together in a passion that didn't need to make sense.

Jeff released the pin from her hair and wound both hands

into her silky tresses, never breaking contact with her lips. He could have stayed like that forever, tasting her, feeling every part of her give in to what they felt together.

Eventually they pulled apart; a small smile played on Eva's lips and Jeff traced it with his fingertip. "So," he said after a moment. "You believe me then?"

She regarded him seriously for a moment before she grinned and said, "Well, any man who can get me on a horse is probably a keeper, don't you think, horse guy?"

He pulled her back in close and matched her grin. "Well, what are we waiting for? Let's go for a ride."

I hope you enjoyed Mistaken Gifts! But the love isn't over yet. I have a special bonus scene just for you! Find out what happened when Jeff and Eva left the Lodge and returned to the city.
Follow along on a special date and very memorable moment.
Read the bonus scene NOW!

Remember that television set Jeff was going to work on? Well...now you can meet Gage Mitchell, the star of that television show and Megan Powers, the PR rep that's been tasked with keeping him out of trouble. Sparks are certainly going to fly between these two in Secret Gifts.

Secret Gifts

Please enjoy an excerpt from Secret Gifts, the next in the Castle Mountain Lodge Series

The moment Megan Powers saw the note on her desk, she knew what it was going to say. And she wasn't going to like it. A memo from her boss, Lois Grace, the head of the Grace Agency, a top Los Angeles PR firm, was almost never a good thing. Especially when that memo was requesting your presence in her office as soon as you got in. Especially when that memo arrived the day after you broke up with her son. The one everyone, including yourself, thought you were going to marry.

Megan dropped her head to her desk, and tried her best to think of what she could say. But it was hard to think on only a few hours sleep, and she'd need a pretty good explanation of why she'd broken Ryan's heart. Better than the "I just don't love you enough" excuse she'd given Ryan himself. But that's only if she knew about it. And how would Lois know about the breakup when it had been less than twenty-four hours? Really, it was hardly even official. There would be no way Lois had heard about it.

Except Megan knew the chances of that were slim. Lois had eyes and ears everywhere. It was eerie how she knew everything all the time, but that was part of what made her so successful with her clients. Most of the time, Lois could figure out what they were going to do before they even did it. Megan hit her head lightly against the desk, trying to figure something out. Despite being omniscient, Lois also had a reputation for being a hard ass. But she was fair, too, and for the last five years that Megan had worked for her, they'd always had a good working relationship. One that was only made stronger when Megan had started dating Ryan, and Lois began talking about a family business and expanding the firm. But that was before she'd crushed her little boy's heart.

"Good morning. Is there some reason you're giving yourself a concussion today?"

Megan jumped up at her assistant Cindy's voice. She smoothed her skirt and rubbed at her forehead where she was sure she'd have a mark.

"Well, you don't have to quit on my account," Cindy said. She snapped her bubble gum as she waltzed into Megan's office with a stack of files and her morning latte. "Here." She handed her the coffee. "Looks like you could use this."

"That bad?"

Cindy nodded and dropped into the chair across from Megan. She blew a big bubble and popped it before flipping open her portfolio.

"You know I hate the gum, right?"

Cindy nodded. It wasn't the first time Megan had mentioned it and if she wasn't such a great assistant, she might have actually done something about it. As it was, some battles weren't worth fighting.

"Hey," Cindy said. "It's the gum or the smokes. I pick

gum." She clicked her pen and poised it over the paper. "So, are you ready to get to work, or what? I have your agenda for the day."

Megan took a sip of her coffee, praying the caffeine worked quickly. She'd done nothing but toss and turn, wondering if she'd made the right decision by breaking up with Ryan. He was sweet and kind. Funny and handsome. Successful and…he was perfect. But not for her. Which was why it'd been so hard. And to watch his face, usually so strong and handsome, crumble when she told him it was over—it was heart wrenching.

But she couldn't change her mind. Despite the hours of talking, and tears from both of them. Ryan wanted to get married. And that wasn't happening. No way.

"Earth to Megan." Cindy was waving a piece of paper in front of her face. "I get that you had a rough night, but you'll get over it and in a few days everyone will stop talking—"

"Wait." Megan snapped to attention. "What are you talking about? A rough night? How did you know and what do you mean, everyone's talking about it?"

Cindy blushed and looked down at her paper where she was furiously drawing circles. "I didn't really say that everyone was talking about it, but—"

"About what?" They knew. Megan's stomach clenched into a knot and squeezed.

"About you and Ryan breaking up," Cindy said and looked at her with pity.

"How does everyone know?" Megan asked despite already knowing the answer. They were a PR firm. Knowing things was their business.

"If it helps, no one is blaming you, not really," Cindy said. "And Ryan isn't in yet. But his assistant said—"

"Stop." Megan held up her hand. "I need to think." She

took another sip of her latte, not caring that the hot liquid burned her tongue.

"I really am sorry," Cindy said. "Is there anything I can do?"

Megan reached across her desk and handed Cindy the memo. "Yes," she said. "Tell me what I should do about this."

Her assistant scanned the note and to her credit, didn't brush it off. Instead, Cindy let out a low whistle. "You think she knows?"

Megan nodded.

"And she's probably not very happy about it either," Cindy added.

"So? What do I do?"

Cindy handed back the note. "If I were you, I wouldn't put it off much longer," she said. "Besides, how bad could it be? Lois is a professional."

Those were the words Megan kept in her head as she walked down the hall. How bad could it be, really? After all, Megan was one of her top agents and that wasn't going to change just because she wasn't going to marry Ryan. She'd continue to do a good job, and they'd continue to work together and everything would be fine.

She'd almost talked herself into believing it by the time she arrived at Lois' office. Her assistant waved her right in as if she'd been expecting her. Which she no doubt was. With a deep breath and a tug at her jacket to pull it into place, Megan walked through the doors.

Lois, blond hair pulled back into a low bun, makeup meticulous, and looking much more like Megan's sister rather than her almost mother-in-law, was reclining in her chair, twirling a pen between her perfectly manicured fingers when Megan walked in.

Megan tucked her own chewed-to-the-nub nails behind her. It was a bad habit she thought she'd broken, until a few hours earlier when she'd walked out of Ryan's living room. "Lois," she said, doing her best to go for calm and relaxed. "Good morning."

"It is," Lois said coolly. "There's nothing quite like a California morning, is there?"

Megan nodded, and gave her a smile. She walked through the room and tried her best to get a read on Lois. Did she know? Was she mad or ready to demand answers out of Megan? She couldn't tell. Lois was practically impossible to read—it was one of her best traits—but at the moment, Megan was finding it exceedingly troubling.

"You wanted to see me, Lois?" Megan sat across from her and crossed her legs. She was careful to make eye contact the way she normally would because she was determined not to let her personal life impact her career with the Grace Agency. She'd worked too damn hard.

"I did," Lois said. "Thank you for coming so early. I know you're very busy, but I thought it important for us to meet right away."

"Absolutely." Megan leaned forward. "Lois, I have to tell you...I didn't intend for—"

"I have a problem, Megan."

"A problem?"

"Yes, I think you're the woman to handle it for me. And it's really quite time sensitive."

"It is?"

"Yes." Lois looked at her strangely. "That's why I called you in this morning, Megan. Did you think it was something else?"

Megan assessed the other woman. It was almost impossible to tell if Lois knew about her and Ryan. She debated for a few moments about saying something. She opened her mouth to tell her. But tell her what? Megan closed her mouth and shook her head. "No," she said finally. "I wasn't sure what you needed to talk about." It wasn't exactly a lie. "So what is this you need my help on?"

Lois narrowed her eyes and let out a long breath. It was in that instant Megan realized she'd been tested, and she'd failed. "I wasn't sure you'd be right for the job until just this moment," Lois said.

Megan tried not to cringe and let her panic show on her face.

"Lois, I—"

"I need you to run damage control with Gage Mitchell."

It took a second for Megan to catch up with what Lois had said. She shook her head. "What?"

"Gage Mitchell," Lois repeated. She clipped her pen and started making notes. "Hollywood's hottest new thing. Star of the summer blockbuster, *Extinction*." She looked up and stared directly into Megan's eyes. "Please tell me you saw it."

Megan nodded. She'd seen it with Ryan. It was the typical blockbuster with shoot 'emup action, and aliens or some such threat to the world and no real story line to speak of. But Gage Mitchell, despite the terrible writing, had somehow risen above and managed to shine against the backdrop of special effects and cars blowing up. There was no doubt, he was the real thing. And it wasn't just his six-pack abs that were a hit with fans. He'd proved he had the skills to make it. "I saw it," she said. "It was…good."

"It was terrible," Lois said. "But Gage was great. And he's also one of the agency's biggest clients right now." She rolled her eyes.

"That's a good thing…" Megan struggled to make the connection with what Lois was saying and what she'd need her for.

"It would be if he wasn't such a huge party boy and a total train wreck right now."

"That's pretty normal," she said with a shrug. "What's the problem?"

"The problem?" Lois slapped both her hands against the desk and leaned forward so she was practically in Megan's personal space. "The problem is that he's one of the Grace Agency's most important clients right now and his party boy ways are going to get him fired from the biggest job of his career if he's not careful."

Megan shook her head. "I don't follow."

"Megan, are you not paying any attention at all to our industry?"

Ouch. That was a hit that hurt and Lois would have known it. Megan's clients were primarily musicians and literary wonders. A completely different species, if you were to ask anyone in the agency. Movie stars were not her specialty. They required a completely different skill set. One that typically involved running interference and handling damage control.

Without giving Megan a chance to respond, Lois said, "Gage has been given the starring role in *Tumbleweed*. It's a new Western series set to premiere in less than a month. It has the top producers, directors, and a supporting cast any show would kill for. The writers are top-notch and there is nothing standing in the way of it becoming a huge hit. Except, of course, for the stars themselves."

"I don't get it, Lois." Megan reclined in her seat. "I mean, he's just doing what he always does. Why should it matter so much?"

"Because, Megan," she said her name with a malice Megan had never heard. "*Tumbleweed* is being billed as a wholesome, all-American show, with heroes kids can relate to, look up to. Something for people to believe in. And if Gage Mitchell insists on keeping up with the party boy image, he'll be in breach of contract."

"That doesn't even—"

"The first season just wrapped, but the producers have already said they'd kill off his character in the premiere and find themselves a new hero if he doesn't pull it together and fast."

Megan sat back and watched Lois, afraid to ask the next question. "I don't understand what this has to do with me," she said after a moment.

"You're going to be the one to make sure he doesn't do anything stupid between now and the premiere," Lois said. "I figure if he can keep his nose out of trouble until the premiere, America will fall in love with his character, Wyatt Dean, and the producers won't be able to afford to kill him off."

"Okay," she said slowly. "I still don't understand what this has to do with me."

"You," Lois pointed a red nail at her, "are going to be the one to make sure he stays out of trouble."

Megan almost laughed, the idea was so funny. "I don't do television stars, Lois."

"You do now."

"But—"

"You'll find your flight information on your desk when you get back."

Megan's head spun. "Flight information? But, where—"

"Canada. The mountains, to be exact," Lois said. She turned to some papers on her desk and started flipping through them. "*Tumbleweed* films in Alberta. It's above Montana."

"I know where Alberta is."

Lois looked up sharply. "Well then," she said. "You'll be familiar with the Rockies, then."

"Of course." Megan didn't like where the conversation was going, or the tone Lois had taken.

"Good. Because I've booked Gage into the Castle Mountain Lodge," Lois said. "He shouldn't be able to get into too much trouble there and the press won't know where to look for him."

Megan shook her head slowly. "I'm not going—"

"You leave in four hours," Lois said. She stood abruptly and pushed her chair back. "Unless you refuse to honor your commitment, of course."

Megan knew what Lois was fishing for. "My commitment to this agency has never wavered, Lois." Megan stood and faced the other woman.

Lois grinned and the look in her eyes made Megan sit again.

It was just a moment, but one long enough for Megan to realize exactly where she stood, before Lois said, "Then I trust you'll enjoy your time in Canada."

His dark aviator glasses couldn't cover the bags under Gage Mitchell's eyes when his driver pulled up at the front doors of Castle Mountain Lodge, but he put them on anyway.

It was better than nothing, and he knew enough even in his hung over state, that his manager, Lucas Stevens, would string him up if he walked into such a classy place looking like he'd partied for three days straight. Even if it was exactly what he'd done.

The door to the car opened and Gage instinctively covered his eyes with his arm. Whatever time it was, it was too early if the sun was still so high in the sky. And not for the first time, a wave of regret washed over him. The pounding head and churning stomach when he woke up wasn't worth it anymore. Not that it ever had been.

When his eyes adjusted to the bright light, Gage got out of the car and took his time looking around. He'd never been up to the mountains before, which seemed ridiculous, but was true. He grew up in a small farming town in the middle of Indiana and all he'd known in his twenty-six years was corn fields.

That was, until that moment when a talent scout found him sitting on his tailgate, eating a burger. After that, things had happened so fast he'd barely had a moment to breathe, let alone look around.

The mountains loomed over him, making Gage dizzy when he tipped his head back and stared. He spun slowly in a circle, taking it all in. Breathing in the fresh air, he filled his lungs. It had been too long since he was out of a big city, away from the buildings, the noise, and the smog. Even filming *Tumbleweed*, just outside of Calgary, wasn't really getting away. Not once you added in all the set pieces, trailers, and equipment.

"Mr. Mitchell?" A voice interrupted his private assessment of his surroundings.

Gage brought his head down, aware of how ridiculous he must look, gaping at the mountains like a child. He cleared his throat and looked at the woman who'd spoken to him. She had dark hair and beautiful green eyes, and while she seemed to be in charge, she clearly looked nervous to be speaking to him. He had that effect on women.

"That's me," he said.

"My name is Carmen Kincaid." She held out her hand and for a split second, Gage considered kissing it, which is something his new persona would do. Instead, he reverted to his upbringing and shook the woman's hand.

"I assume you're my new babysitter?" He couldn't help the sarcasm that crept into his voice.

The woman's face hardened and she withdrew her hand. "Why you need a babysitter is your own business, Mr. Mitchell. But I am the manager of guest relations here at the Lodge and it's my job to make sure you have everything you need."

Shame flooded through him. "Well, I'm sure you'll do a

good job," he said, and instantly regretted his choice of words. He glanced around for the cloud of paparazzi that followed him wherever he went. That little statement said to a beautiful woman would be eaten up by the press. "That's not how I meant it," he added quickly. "I mean, I—"

"It's fine, Mr. Mitchell." Carmen's face opened in a bright smile. "I know how you meant it. And don't worry," she added. "There aren't any cameras up here. I worked closely with the Grace Agency to be sure no one knew you were coming."

Gage took another look around. Besides the spectacular scenery that was the notable feature, there were no photographers. The endless parade of reporters that hounded him for any shred of scandal or misstep. And hadn't he done a good job fuelling their fire? "It is quiet," Gage said after a moment.

"You'll find the Lodge to be one of the most peaceful places you've ever been to. There will, of course, be other guests who will no doubt recognize you, but with any luck, we can keep the press away. And for the protection of all our guests, we've lowered the gate and added extra security."

"I'm sure everything will be fine," Gage said. He took another look around. Lucas had been looking to keep him out of trouble, and by the looks of the place he'd found for him to hide, there wouldn't be any trouble he could get into. It was perfect.

He flashed Carmen one of his killer smiles and she blushed.

"Why don't I show you your accommodations, Mr. Mitchell?"

He followed Carmen into the main Lodge and tried to maintain his cool, detached demeanor. But it was hard when all he wanted to do was revert to his country boy roots. The place was amazing and unlike anything he'd ever seen with the rough timber beams along the vaulted ceiling and the oversized river rock fireplace that was the centerpiece of the room.

"What do you think?" Carmen turned and asked.

He hadn't realized he'd stopped walking. He cleared his throat and said, "It should do."

Carmen eyed him strangely, but didn't say anything. "Most of our guests like it," she said.

Dropping the persona he'd worked so hard to create, he smiled an honest smile and said, "It really is beautiful. I've never seen anything quite like it."

She smiled, obviously satisfied. "Well, let's get you checked in and you can explore everything Castle Mountain has to offer. I think you'll like it."

Gage smiled and for the first time in longer than he could remember, it was his own, honest smile. "I think you're right," he said.

He followed her to the front desk and quickly scrawled his signature. Lucas and his PR agency had taken care of most of the registration details. No doubt trying to make his exile as painless as possible. If only they knew the truth. The moment they told him about it, and after he got over the initial shock of being told what to do, he'd been looking forward to it.

"And I think that's all we need," Carmen said, when he slid the paper across the desk to her. "If you'd like, I can show you to your suite. We were told there'd be one other person joining you."

Gage tried not to roll his eyes. "That would be my latest PR rep."

"Oh yes, the babysitter you referred to earlier?"

Gage almost laughed at her perceptiveness. "That's the one. And whoever it is they found for me this time won't be joining me," he added. As if he was going to share a room with whatever agent they'd stuck him with after the last incident. "You'll have to get them their own room."

He saw the indecision cross her face, but she smiled and said, "Well, I'm sure we can—"

"Carmen, who's your new friend?"

Gage turned to see a beautiful blond woman wearing a uniform matching Carmen's. He gave her his trademark smile and lowered his sunglasses just enough to make eye contact, but not enough for her to see how bloodshot his eyes really were. "Well, hello," he said. "The name is Gage." He held out his hand.

"Gage Mitchell?" the blond asked with a giggle. "Well, it certainly is nice to meet you." She flipped her hair back and gave him what he recognized to be an inviting smile. He'd seen enough women in Los Angeles with that exact look on their face. Unfortunately for the women, it had the opposite of the desired effect on Gage. He'd seen it too many times.

He glanced over at Carmen and tried not to laugh at the look she was making where the blond couldn't see.

"Lisa," Carmen said. "As you know, this is Gage Mitchell. He'll be staying here for a while. As discreetly as possible," she added.

"Oh," Lisa purred. "I get it. Your secret is safe with me." She batted her eyes in a way that he was sure was designed to make men do stupid things.

"Nice to meet you, Lisa." Gage didn't want to be rude, but he also didn't want to give her the wrong impression. It wasn't worth it. "I'm sure I'll see you around."

"I'm sure you will." She ran her hand along his arm in a move that even he had to admit was bold. "It can get pretty quiet up here at night, but I happen to know a few things going on that will spice it up."

"I bet you do."

For a moment, Gage let himself get caught up in the web she was weaving. Old habits were hard to break. And she was beautiful, and clearly wanted to show him a good time and—

"I don't think Mr. Mitchell is going to be very interested in anything spicy, Lisa."

"Oh, I don't know," Gage said before he could stop himself. "I've been known to enjoy a little spice from time to time."

"That's what I hear." Lisa slipped a little closer to him, until she was very much in his personal space. Gage knew he should pull away. Nothing good would come from getting involved with her.

He took her hand in his and lifted it from her arm. "Thank you, Lisa. But for right now, I think I'm going to spend some time getting to know the Lodge."

Gage released her hand and let it drop gently before turning to Carmen. "Thank you for your help, Carmen. I'll find my own way to the suite. I think I need a bit of fresh air first."

Carmen nodded and handed him his keys and a map of the grounds. "Remember, Mr. Mitchell. If there's anything you need, please don't hesitate."

What he needed was space and time to think about the mess he'd made of his life. But something told him the women standing in front of him weren't going to be able to help with either of those things. He managed a smile and turned to walk away.

He was only a few steps away when he heard Carmen hiss at the other woman. "Lisa, we promised Mr. Mitchell's people he'd have a nice relaxing visit here. No parties. No drama. Now, cut it out."

"Lighten up. How often do you get a gorgeous movie star so close? Besides, you can promise his people anything you want, but isn't it about what he wants?"

Gage sighed and kept walking. That was the million dollar question. Wasn't it about what he wanted? And even if it was, what if he had no idea what it was he really wanted?

Gage followed his map and it led him to a pathway circuit that ran along the ridge of the mountains, and looked down below the valley. According to his map, there should be at least fifteen kilometers of interweaving pathways. The sun was shining and and the spring air was warm, but there was still a bit of a chill in the air so far up in the mountains. Just enough to remind you that summer was still a few months away.

Gage strolled through the trees, letting his mind clear and pretty soon his headache was gone and he could think a little clearer.

If he was still on set, he'd be in bed early, ready to film the next day. Despite his well-deserved reputation as a party boy, he took his work seriously. And he wouldn't jeopardize it, not for anything. Gage refused to be one of those actors who showed up hung over, or worse yet, still drunk, and couldn't remember their lines or caused a big scene. No, when it was time to work, he was all business. Stardom had come too easily, and he couldn't afford for it to be taken away.

The ringing of his cell phone shattered the quiet of the day. He didn't even have to look at it to know who it was, but he answered it anyway.

"Lucas," Gage said. "I suppose you're calling to make sure I'm still alive?" He couldn't keep the bitter tone from his voice.

"Gage, don't be like that," Lucas said. "You know I only want what's best for you."

A year ago, Gage might have believed that to be true, but more and more he was having trouble identifying the people in his life who actually cared.

"Well, I'm not drunk, there are no women in my bed, and I'm being every bit the model citizen you want me to be." He kept walking while he listened to Lucas ramble on about how sending him to the mountains was best for his image and it was crucial in his career to present himself a certain way and other things. Gage basically stopped listening to him.

"Are you listening to me?"

Gage rolled his eyes. "Of course," he said.

"Good. Because I don't think you realize how serious things

are. The producers of *Tumbleweed* are not impressed. If you pull another stunt like the other night, they're going to kill off your character before the show even airs. Do you know what that means?"

He did know what it meant. It meant he'd be kissing goodbye to the best role he'd ever had.

"Yes," he said.

"Then cut it out, Gage." His manager and friend raised his voice. Gage knew Lucas was frustrated with him; hell, he was frustrated with himself. "Stop screwing it up. All you have to do is stay out of trouble for a few weeks. Do you think you can do that?"

Gage nodded. He could, if that was what he wanted. "I can," he said after a moment. "But you're sending me a babysitter to make sure I do, is that right?"

"The agency insisted," Lucas said. "And I don't think it's a bad idea." The other man sighed. "Look, Gage. I don't know what's going on with you, but take this time and figure it out, okay? Do not sabotage everything you've worked for."

Sabotage? Gage had never had anyone come right out and put a name on what it was he was doing. And Lucas probably didn't even realize how close to the truth he'd come.

"Fine," he agreed. "I'll lie low."

Will Megan be able to keep Gage under control? Or will they make each other crazy? Find out and read the rest of Secret Gifts NOW!

About the Author

Elena Aitken is a USA Today Bestselling Author of more than forty romance and women's fiction novels. The mother of 'grown up' twins, Elena now lives with her very own mountain man in the heart of the very mountains she writes about. She can often be found with her toes in the lake and a glass of wine in her hand, dreaming up her next book and working on her own happily ever after.

To learn more about Elena:
www.elenaaitken.com
elena@elenaaitken.com